A SINGLE SOUL

L.A. WITT

Copyright Information

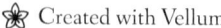 Created with Vellum

ARTIFICIAL INTELLIGENCE

No artificial intelligence was used in the making of this book or any of my books. This includes writing, co-writing, cover artwork, translation, and audiobook narration.

I do not consent to any Artificial Intelligence (AI), generative AI, large language model, machine learning, chatbot, or other automated analysis, generative process, or replication program to reproduce, mimic, remix, summarize, train from, or otherwise replicate any part of this creative work, via any means: print, graphic, sculpture, multimedia, audio, or other medium. This applies to all existing AI technology and any that comes into existence in the future.

I support the right of humans to control their artistic works.

*To Michael Ferraiuolo, who sent me an email starting with
"Hey, here's a plot bunny..."
Just remember when you're narrating it that you brought this
on yourself.*

ABOUT A SINGLE SOUL

Matt Russo knows better. Everyone does, but no one knows better than an attorney who routinely works with the fae: you watch what you say, or else you find yourself in the crosshairs of trickster magic.

Or in this case, with an angel on one shoulder and a demon on the other. And the ridiculous bickering celestial beings aren't going anywhere until they help him change his perpetual single status. Worse, if someone finds out he used magic for any kind of gain, his personal and professional reputations might never recover.

Fortunately, his best friend and downstairs neighbor— not to mention the man he's quietly wanted for the past five years—is smart and level-headed. If anyone can help Matt out of this fiasco, it's Cory Miller.

Except while Cory's happy to help Matt get rid of the pint-sized magical idiots, the only way they're leaving is if they succeed in finding someone for Matt to love. Cory will do anything for his friend, but he's not so sure he can take part in helping Matt find the man of his dreams. Not when he's wished all this time that *he* could fill that particular role.

But maybe this magical disaster is exactly what Matt and Cory need to realize their secret attraction is mutual.

A Single Soul is approximately 40,000 words.

CHAPTER 1

MATT

I... did not think this through.

And damn it, I knew better. You don't spend fifteen years representing fae, sorcerers, and the odd alchemist in the courtroom without learning to be *very* careful about every word you say. Otherwise you ended up like that district attorney—his name escapes me right now—whose political aspirations went up in smoke because he got careless and gave his name to a trickster who was now a U.S. senator running for reelection.

So. Yeah. I knew better.

In my admittedly weak defense, I was desperate. Everyone thinks they're *so smart* and would *never* fall for trickster magic, but let's see how rational and responsible *you* are when your love life is so pathetic that Spirit Halloween wants to rent out one side of your bed.

Staring into my bathroom mirror now, I rewound the events of the last few days, trying to figure out how exactly I'd ended up here.

Or rather, how *they'd* ended up here—"they" being the two tiny beings perched on my shoulders.

On the left, a demon. On the right, an angel. I supposed I should be thankful the angel wasn't one of the Old Testament angels with the dozens of eyes and however many wings. I'd had a little too much to drink last night to process that. Not that I was doing such a hot job of getting all *this* into my head.

I wiped a hand over my unshaven face, then glared at my two passengers. "Okay, now that I'm... Maybe 'awake' is being generous, but..." I gestured dismissively. "Just... run it all by me again?"

In an instant, they were talking over each other, both sounding entirely too conscious and—at least in the angel's case—perky for 7:43 on a Saturday morning.

"One at a time," I growled.

They quieted and leaned forward to look past me at each other. I watched in the mirror as they gestured and shrugged in a pantomime of *"You want to? No, you do it."*

I rolled my eyes. Then I pointed sharply at the angel. "You."

He jumped and stammered, "Oh. Uh. I..." After a second, he recovered, pushed his shoulders back, and spoke, his accent British and his voice a *little* too loud, given the night I'd spent with Jack Daniels. "We've been sent here to assist you in finding a companion."

I blinked. They'd both said as much when I'd first discovered them, but I'd been so freaked the hell out because hello—a tiny angel and demon? What the fuck? Now that I'd calmed down... no, it didn't make any more sense than it had during my initial panic.

"Assist me. In finding a companion." I shook my head. "What the fuck does that even—"

The demon huffed, and he sounded Scottish and bored:

"What my feather-brained colleague means is that we're here to get you laid."

I eyed him as much as my throbbing head would allow. "So you're my divine wingmen?"

The angel made an indignant sound. "I am *not* a winged man. I am an *angel*."

"Oh, for fuck's sake." The demon rubbed his hand over his face much like I had a moment ago. "He didn't mean— mortals call someone a wingman if they help them get laid. Do you even *read* the briefings?"

"I do read them!"

"Do you, though?" The demon's voice dripped with sarcasm. "Because on our last assignment, you thought Grindr was a power tool."

Annnd just like that, they were bickering again, flailing arms, wings, and—I thought—a tail at the edges of my peripheral vision as they shouted past me.

I rubbed my eyes. This was a dream, right? I'd had a little too much to drink last night, and I was still sound asleep in my bed, hallucinating vividly about two mosquitoes buzzing around my head.

This was absolutely not reality. It definitely wasn't a consequence of visiting a former client from the Fae District and asking if her whole matchmaking thing actually worked. Or of her smiling sweetly and asking, face and voice full of innocence, if I needed help finding a companion.

I stared at the angel. At the demon.

At my loud, obnoxious, bickering wingmen.

Oh, fuck my life.

That loud, obnoxious bickering wasn't helping my throbbing head, so I barked, "Hey!"

That also didn't help, but it did have the desired effect:

they both fell silent. I was pretty sure the demon almost fell *off*, too, but he recovered his dignity, if one could call it that, and perched on my shoulder with his feet resting on my collarbone like he owned the place.

"I don't suppose I can say, 'no thanks' and send you guys back to... uh... wherever?"

In the mirror, two tiny heads shook. The angel looked vaguely sympathetic. The demon looked highly amused.

Goddammit. You knew you were fucked when you were a lawyer and didn't know a single argument or loophole to help you weasel out of a situation. I was way too well-versed in fae law to think I could technicality my way out of this.

I pressed my hands onto the cool edges of the sink and gave a resigned sigh. "Okay. Fine. What are the rules, then? How does this work?" I paused. "And are you guys just... always here until this is over?"

They both looked at me stupidly in the mirror.

"Where else would we be?" the angel asked.

"Um." Okay, that was a fair question. "I don't know? Somewhere other than..." I motioned at my shoulders. "Like do you take breaks? Do I get privacy?" I inclined my head. "Are you guys going to stick around until I finish getting laid? Because that might, uh... not help the situation."

The angel rubbed his chin.

The demon groaned and seemed to roll his eyes—he was pretty small and my own eyes ached too much to focus —and then reached into the inside pocket of his black jacket. From there, he produced what I thought was a piece of parchment, and he peered at it as gingerly as if he were as hungover as I was. "Right. Right. Something, something, legalese..." He huffed and rolled his free hand as he apparently skimmed to the pertinent clause. "Ah! 'Upon signee's request, or no less than twice per day at assistants' requests, the assistants will depart aforementioned signee's presence for periods not to exceed fifteen minutes...' blah, blah, blah..." He tilted his head from side to side as he kept reading, mumbling to himself, "Christ, can't they ever write this shite in *English?*"

The angel huffed. "Says the Scot."

"Hey! Sod off!"

"I beg your pardon?"

I pinched the bridge of my nose. "Would someone just answer my damn question? Can you guys wait to argue until ..." For fuck's sake. Did this contract really include state-mandated fifteen-minute breaks for them? Then again, that gave me fifteen minutes of privacy, so I probably shouldn't bitch. "Argue on your own time," I growled. "And that's it? Just... fifteen-minute increments a few times a day?"

The demon kept reading. He flipped to a second page and muttered to himself. Something about more legalese and just getting to the bloody point already.

The angel cupped his elbow and stroked his chin thoughtfully. "Doesn't it say we'll depart if he makes a connection with someone?"

I lifted my eyebrows. That sounded promising.

"Aye, it does." The demon nodded. "The assistants and —" He waved a hand and lowered the agreement. "The English version is that when it looks like you're about to get laid, we're gone."

The angel made an indignant sound. "It most certainly does not say something so crass."

The demon waved the parchment pages. "Says the birdbrain who obviously doesn't read the contracts *or* the briefings."

The angel's indignation intensified to the point I swore it made that ear ring, but I spoke before he could.

"Okay, okay, but how exactly am I supposed to connect with someone if I've got..." I gestured at each of them.

More confusion. More poring over the tiny parchment.

I swore under my breath and rubbed my eyes again. How the hell was I supposed to connect with someone like this? Because nothing said *"look how stable and put together I am"* like unavoidable evidence you'd resorted to *magic*. For anything. It was unattractive, undesirable, and un—

"Oh shit!" I straightened suddenly, barely noticing the way that made my head throb. "*Can* other people see you?"

The angel looked contemplative. The demon looked confused.

"Let me guess," I grumbled. "You don't know that either?"

They both shook their heads. The demon kept looking though the parchment, still shaking his head.

Oh no. Oh fuck.

"I can't go to work like this!" My voice came out shrill and panicked. Which... I mean... the shoe fit. "Do you know what this will do to my reputation? I have two depositions this week! And I have to be in *court* on—I can't just... Oh, Jesus Christ."

"No, no." The angel shook his head again. "He's not involved in any of this."

The demon facepalmed. I concurred.

And I still didn't have an answer. I mean, what did I have to do? Just... venture out and see if anyone saw my ridiculous companions? Ugh. God help me if they did. The last thing I needed was to advertise to the whole world—and all my colleagues and clientele—that I'd stupidly asked a fae for help, and that was exactly what everyone would assume when they saw this shitshow. What other explanation could there be?

If someone did see me—if they saw this angel and demon on my shoulders—that would be a disaster. A professional and personal one that I couldn't afford and was way worse than being depressingly single. I couldn't have the stigma that came with using magic to get what I wanted. I'd worked hard for my professional reputation, and if it got out that I'd used magic for literally anything, then everything I'd ever done or achieved would be called into question. My law degree, my partnership at one of those most prestigious firms in the state, the athletic medals and trophies I'd won over the years—everyone would wonder if I'd used magic to get those, too.

God, what a mess.

And even without the stigma, these two were allegedly going to help me find a man? But how was that supposed to work? How was I even supposed to leave the house? And how the hell did I connect with someone when I had these two morons flitting around above my shoulders? Wait until their fifteen-minute breaks to make my move?

Over and over, I kept landing on the same unanswered and panic-filled question: what was I supposed to do now?

Fortunately, I had someone nearby who I could go to in a crisis, even if it was a stupid crisis of my own stupid making.

CHAPTER 2

CORY

As luck would have it, I was mid-sip when someone pounded on my front door.

"Damn it," I muttered as I tried to brush hot coffee off my hand, my face, and my shirt, all while trying not to drop the mug. And who was at my door this early on a Saturday morning, anyway? Because the missionaries usually waited until at least nine or ten, and they were a bit more polite about knocking. This kind of loud, demanding sound didn't usually herald *"Do you have some time to talk about your Lord and Savior?"*

Whoever it was, they banged on the door again. Great. They must've been selling something *really* important.

"Just a minute!" I barked. Then I muttered, "Son of a... Who the fuck?" Still wiping coffee off my hand, I strode down the hall to the front door.

There was yet another knock a split second before I turned the deadbolt, which nearly prompted a cranky, "Well, fuck you, then." But I don't know—now that I thought about it, the knocking sounded less demanding and more... frantic?

As concern chased away my annoyance, I opened the door. "What in the—"

"Oh, thank God." Matt, my best friend and upstairs neighbor, stared at me with wide, panicked eyes. "I need your help."

My pulse surged with panic of my own. Matt was one of the most level-headed people I'd ever met. It wasn't just because he was a lawyer, either. My ex's dad had been a lawyer and he'd been anything but level-headed. So seeing Matt like this—freaking out and pleading for help—was alarming to say the least.

"Uh. Okay. Okay. You—my help? What? With—"

But then my teeth snapped shut. Because I realized Matt hadn't come alone.

I flicked my gaze from his right shoulder to his left to his right again. Were they... Was I hallucinating? Was there really a pair of—

"So you see them too?" Matt's shoulders dropped beneath his two passengers. The angel was hovering gracefully, but the demon had been perched on top of Matt's shoulder, and he squawked as he damn near tumbled off. With a few flaps of his leathery red wings, he too was upright, floating above Matt's shirt, tugging at his own jacket sleeves as if to reclaim his dignity.

What... in the holy...

I shook myself. "Uh. Yeah. Yeah, I see them, too." I met Matt's gaze. "What's going on?"

His shoulders fell even more, and he sounded more helpless and crestfallen than I'd ever heard him. "I fucked up."

I nodded, still stunned, and stepped aside, gesturing for him to come in. "Okay. All right. Just, uh... Let's sit down and see if we can figure this out?"

The breath he released as he stepped into my apartment was full of relief. Did he think I was going to magically have all the answers? Or had he thought I was going to turn him away? I hoped he hadn't believed I'd slam the door in his face. He had to know me better than that.

Then again, he was clearly in full-on freakout mode, so he might not have been thinking as rationally as he did under normal circumstances. It probably wouldn't hurt to cut him some slack.

I shut the door and followed him into my living room, where he'd started pacing in front of my coffee table.

"I don't know what to do." He flailed a hand. "I've got two depositions this week. And I've got client meetings, and I mean, I can't just walk into the firm or *a fucking courtroom* like..." He gestured sharply at the pair, nearly smacking the demon in the process.

"Okay, okay." I put up my hands. "Slow down for a second." I took a seat on the armrest of the couch. "How, um... How exactly did this happen?"

He stopped pacing and rubbed the back of his neck as he stared at the carpet.

From over his right shoulder, the angel spoke up, fluttering his wings and smiling brightly as he said, "Oh, I do believe I can explain!"

Matt and the demon said in unison, "No."

The angel glared at both of them, folded his arms, and muttered something I didn't catch. If Matt hadn't been so upset, the scene would've been comical. But it was hard to laugh when my friend was hanging by a fraying thread.

Matt started pacing again, rubbing a hand over his scruffy and somewhat pale face. "I should never have let that client take me out to dinner."

"Client?"

But then some pieces clicked. Matt represented a lot of magic users in his practice, especially fae. And this? I didn't know the how or the why, but it *had* to be fae. I could feel it in my bones. Only a trickster could get past Matt's carefully honed defenses, and only a fae would've come up with... that.

I worked in the Fae District myself, so I heard and saw a lot of weird shit. People made careless requests of the fae, not thinking about every imaginable way their words could be interpreted. That was how they ended up getting their identities stolen—like seriously, how many times do people need to be told to never give their name to a fae? I mean, it kept me in business, since my entire career revolved around helping people start new lives with new identities after they stupidly—and legally—gave their name to a fae. I paid my bills via people's carelessness with tricksters.

And so did Matt, which was why I was so surprised he'd fallen for whatever the hell his client had done. He had to have known that wouldn't end well. It never did. Though an actual angel and devil on someone's shoulders? That was... new.

"Okay." I folded my hands in my lap. "One thing at a time. Did you... Did you actually accept food from a fae?"

"No, no." He waved that away. "I might be stupid enough to"—he gestured at his winged companions—"but it was at a restaurant, and I told her I wasn't coming unless we split the check."

I nodded as he spoke. "So, what happened?"

Matt made a miserable sound and sank onto the couch. Pressing his elbows into his knees, he covered his face with both hands. "I had *way* too much to drink. And then she asked how in the world I was single."

I grimaced. So did the angel. The demon might've too,

but I couldn't see him as well from where I was sitting. Honestly, I'd wondered that a number of times, too. Not enough to discuss it in the company of a fae, though I wouldn't lie—in a moment or two of weakness, I had been tempted to ask a fae to help me turn his head and win his heart. But I didn't, because love magic was just manipulative awfulness that I wanted no part of. I didn't want Matt unless it was mutual. And after five years of close friendship... Well. It wasn't happening without magic or divine intervention, so it wasn't happening at all.

Shame. He was the sweetest and smartest man I'd ever met. When he'd had boyfriends, I'd coveted those soft smiles and gentle touches. Even now I was tempted to make a deal with the fae—or with the Devil himself—just to be on the receiving end of one of those longing, heartfelt looks he gave a man he loved.

Matt wasn't hard on the eyes, either. He had a few years on me—forty-three to my thirty-five—and he was just... God, he was hot. Right now, he was just wearing jeans and an old T-shirt, and he rocked that look the same way he did those bespoke suits he wore to work. Time, genes, and law school had started turning his near-black hair silver. Sharp blue eyes melted my brain whenever he met my gaze and melted my heart whenever he was smiling. One laugh from him could scramble my thoughts for days.

And seeing him like this... Fuck, it broke my heart. Even if he had stupidly brought it on himself.

I wanted to grab him by the broad, perfect shoulders and shake him as I said, *"It's the fae, Matt! The fucking fae! What did you* think *would happen?"*

But I didn't. Because he was a wreck right now, and he was coming to me for help out of a mess he was already in. Kicking him while he was down wouldn't help anyone.

"So, you got drunk with your fae client," I said gently. "And she asked about you being single." I inclined my head. "Then what?"

Matt lowered his hands and sat back, staring miserably at the opposite wall as the angel and demon fluttered on either side of his head. "I just... I don't know. I guess I got drunk enough to start yammering on about it, and how I was so fucking done being single, and then—" He stopped, expression suddenly sharpening, and he tensed as if he were having some kind of revelation.

I moved from the armrest to the cushion, though I left some space between us. "What?"

Matt swallowed. As he closed his eyes and swore, some color rose in his otherwise pale cheeks. He swallowed hard before turning to me, his expression full of embarrassment. "I asked her if that matchmaking magic really works."

"Oh, no," I breathed.

"Yeah." He sighed with defeat and despair. "Oh, fuck me."

"He could!" The angel pointed at me. "Then the spell would be broken and—"

"Oh my God," Matt groaned, turning even redder. "No."

My teeth snapped shut, and I was pretty sure I was blushing too; that heat was pretty unmistakable. Every time someone joked about the two of us getting together—and our friends were *relentless* about it—I died a little inside because I wished we could, and because of Matt's predictable response.

"He's a *friend*," he growled at the angel. "I'm not going to sleep with him just to get rid of the two of you."

I mean... at least he wasn't going to ask me for a pity fuck. I'd sleep with him in a heartbeat, but only if he *wanted* me. Not in the name of being-be-gone. No matter how much those beings were clearly stressing him out.

Desperate for some levity to distract from the sudden focus on Matt and me getting into bed, I chanced a smirk. "So you asked a fae—one you've had to represent over her shady practices—about matchmaking?" I snorted. "Did you fae around and find out?"

Matt rolled his eyes. "Really?"

"What?" I chuckled. "I'm just saying. You of all people know better than to ask a fae for something. Especially one who's needed *your* help."

To my great relief, he managed a halfhearted laugh, too. "Please. What magic wielder hasn't needed a lawyer at some point?"

"Eh, okay, fair." I cleared my throat, trying to collect my dignity and not make this any worse for him. At least we weren't talking about us fucking anymore. "Do they, uh…" I gestured at his winged friends. "Do they have names?"

"Um. I didn't… I didn't ask."

"No, you didn't," the demon said indignantly. "It's just been 'what the fuck are you?' and 'what the fuck is going on?'" He huffed. "Can't even be bothered to ask what our fucking names are."

"Really?" The angel leaned past Matt's head. "*Must* you curse so much?"

"Of course I must! I'm a fucking demon!"

The angel seemed to consider that, then said, "He does make a compelling argument."

"He does." Matt exhaled, peering at the demon but then apparently thinking better of it. Probably because he was, I assumed, hungover. Looking that closely at anything must've hurt. Sounding defeated and miserable, he asked, "What are your names, anyway?"

The angel straightened, smiling broadly and puffing out his chest as if he were about to deliver some kind of grand speech.

But the demon spoke first: "I'm Andras. The feathered wankstain is called Raziel."

The angel—Raziel, apparently—deflated and crossed his arms.

"Andras and Raziel." Matt rubbed his face again. "Glad we've all been..." He paused, then gestured at me. "He's Cory, by the way."

"Pleasure to make your acquaintance," Raziel said.

Andras just gave a sarcastic wave.

I... had no idea how to respond. Maybe because I hadn't had enough coffee to process that I was being introduced to a tiny angel and a tiny demon at the same time I was trying to help my friend sort out a crisis.

I shifted on the couch. "So she told you about her matchmaking magic."

Nodding, Matt grimaced. "The rest of the conversation is..." He chewed his lip. "I was drunk, so..."

So he didn't remember. Got it.

I sat straighter. "Wait, doesn't that mean the contract is null and void? If you can't remember agreeing to it? Or even what the terms are?"

Matt pursed his lips. Then he shook his head. "Unless she'll voluntarily rescind it, I'm pretty well fucked."

"Why?"

"Because in order to push the issue, I'd have to file something formal. There'd have to be a hearing. In a courtroom."

"Ooh." I sagged back against the cushion. "Yeah. That... complicates things, doesn't it?"

"Just a bit." Matt made an unhappy sound. "Fuck. I

have court next week! I can't walk into the courtroom like..."
He gestured wildly at Andras and Raziel. "Like *this!*"

"No, no, you can't." I patted the air. "Let's... Why don't
we go see her? Maybe she'd be willing to negotiate something else."

"We?"

"Well, yes." I inclined my head. "Unless you want to
handle this alone?"

Matt chewed his lip, looking unusually sheepish and
vulnerable. "No. I'd rather not."

"Right. So. We."

"Thanks." He smiled flicker fast, then sighed. "Ugh, I
don't imagine any new deal will land in my favor."

"Probably not. But maybe you can live with those terms
instead of... um..." I gestured at my own shoulders.

Matt glanced at each of his tiny companions. Then he
sighed and pushed himself up off the couch. "Let me go
make myself a little more presentable."

"All right." I got up too. "Let me get some coffee. I'll
drive."

CHAPTER 3

MATT

Cory did end up driving, but we took my car. Suddenly those tinted windows I'd splurged on didn't seem so pretentious. Not when they blocked Raziel and Andras from view. And I couldn't exactly tell them to take their fifteen-minute break because they'd done that while I'd been getting dressed.

"I don't see what the big deal is," Raziel said indignantly after I explained that to Cory. "We saw it all while you were sleeping last night."

Andras gave a snarky little chuckle. "He just doesn't want to listen to you talkin' about his willy again." Then, in a high-pitched voice and a badly imitated version of Raziel's accent, he added, "Wouldja lookit that, Andras? I had no idea the hair down there turned gray, too!"

Beside me, Cory snorted, though to his credit, he at least tried to muffle it. When I shot him a glare, he managed a not terribly sincere, "Sorry."

I just rolled my eyes.

"What?" Raziel still sounded as indignant as ever. "I've never seen gray hair down—"

"Okay, okay." I put up my hands. "No more discussing anything you guys saw while I was asleep, all right?"

They both grumbled. Cory suppressed another laugh. And I thanked whoever was listening that I'd been able to send them on a "break" while I'd taken a shower.

"So. Um." Cory cleared his throat and shifted a little in the driver seat. "Where exactly am I going?"

"Do you know where the Unseelie Building is?"

He shot me a wide-eyed look.

"Don't worry—we're not going there." I motioned vaguely ahead. "Her office is across the street. It has a parking garage, too. I'll point it out when we get there."

Cory exhaled. I didn't blame him. There was nothing overly sinister or dangerous about the Unseelie Building. Like all the fae, the Unseelies were required by treaties to abide by human law, and they generally wouldn't fuck with anyone who didn't fuck with them first. But if a rogue fae *was* inclined to fuck with someone unprovoked, they would almost certainly be an Unseelie. Most of us treated them as respectfully as we did any of the other magic beings living among us, but anyone with any sense of self-preservation regarded the Unseelies with the same sense of caution we did goblins and that one clan of particularly antisocial ogres: don't harass them, don't confront them, and—most relevantly here—don't go wandering through their territory uninvited or unescorted.

"Have you, uh..." Cory glanced at me. "Have you ever gone into the Unseelie Building?"

I nodded. "I represented a changeling a couple of years ago, and I went to his office a few times to discuss the case."

"Really?"

"Mmhmm. It was... I don't remember all the details, but he had a dispute with a couple of fauns running a travel agency, and his schedule didn't allow him to come to me as often as I could come to him." I half-shrugged. "It wasn't as big a deal as people make it out to be. Probably because everyone who saw me knew I was there to help one of their own, so they left me alone."

"Oh. Yeah, I guess that makes sense." He adjusted his grip on the wheel. "I probably wouldn't be very popular there."

I studied him. "Why's that?"

Cory laughed softly. "Dude, I make my living helping people who've had their identities stolen by tricksters. Sometimes that includes getting law enforcement and the legal system involved." He grimaced. "Not exactly a line of work that endears me to that crowd."

"Eh. You'd be surprised."

Cory shot me a look before facing the road.

I chuckled. "They're tricksters, but they're not—well, *most* of them aren't evil. Hell, some of the fae I've represented clients against have ended up hiring me themselves later. They see lawyers kind of like they do salespeople and evangelists—people who perform trickster magic without the magic."

"That sounds like a bit of a backhanded compliment."

"It keeps me in the good graces of most of the fae, so..."

"Okay, I can see that. You have to exploit loopholes and technicalities—I can imagine the fae respect that."

"They do." I laughed softly. "Even when they're on the receiving end of it, they respect it."

"Huh. You really do know your way around the tricksters, don't you?"

My humor faded. "You wouldn't know it, given my current situation."

Cory didn't say anything right away. I half-expected

Andras or Raziel to chime in, but they seemed to be preoc-
cupied. Andras was once again poring over a piece of parchment that I assumed was a copy of the agreement. Or
maybe it was the briefing he'd accused Raziel of neglecting
to read. I don't know. Raziel, meanwhile, had moved from
my shoulder to just below the window, and he currently
had his hands and faced pressed to the glass like a child
peering into a toy store. I couldn't imagine this was his first
time seeing a city. Maybe his first time in *this* city? Well,
whatever—I didn't even mind if he left tiny handprints on
the window as long as he wasn't chattering in my ear.

After a block or so of silence, Cory took a breath and
glanced across the console at me. "I don't blame you,
honestly."

That was unexpected. "Really? For getting drunk with
a fae and scoring myself a pair of..." I motioned toward
Andras and Raziel.

"I mean..." Cory shrugged. "Okay, fine, you could've
gone into it differently. But like... I get it, you know?"

I tilted my head. "You do?"

"Well, yeah." Some color rose in his cheeks, and he
breathed a quiet laugh. "I've been single almost as long as
you have. It fucking sucks."

I chewed my lip. This was one of those moments when I
realized how little sense the entire world actually made.
How in hell was Cory alone? I could give a laundry list of
reasons why I totally understood my own inability to land a
partner. My less than sparkling personality. The endless
hours of my demanding job. That whole thing where I was
a partner at my own law firm but couldn't afford to buy a
house because on top of a mountain of student debt, my ex-
husband was a better lawyer than I was and had taken my
ass to the proverbial cleaners.

But I was mystified that *Cory* was still single. He was cute as hell, of course, but he was also one of the sweetest people I'd ever met. The fact that he was patiently driving my stupid ass over to the Fae District this early on a Saturday morning underscored how willing he was to help his friends, even when they'd put themselves into ridiculous situations. I adored how much his quick wit could catch me off-guard with a perfectly timed punchline. The fae thought my work in the courtroom was trickster craft? They'd all be in awe if they ever tried to hold on to their train of thought when he gave one of those spectacular smiles. Or maybe that was just me, though I doubted it. I'd seen him smile and trip up friends, waitstaff, bartenders—even that one cranky cop who'd been about to write him a parking ticket.

If there was any human in this car working actual magic, it sure as shit wasn't me.

And my mind had spun out just thinking about how absurd it was that no one had snatched him up.

I shook myself, prompting a yelp from Andras, who I'd dislodged. As the demon righted himself amidst some more swearing, I said to Cory, "Have you been looking? I, uh... I thought you were staying single for a while. On purpose." God, I was rambling.

"I was. After Ryan, I needed a break from men."

I grunted in agreement. Hell, *I'd* needed a break from men after that fuckknuckle.

"It's been almost two years, though," Cory went on. "I've had enough of hookups. I'm so damn ready to actually be with someone, you know?" He sighed heavily. "Just... haven't had any luck."

"Wow," I said. "That sucks."

He nodded but said nothing. I chewed the inside of my cheek and, like him, stared out the windshield. I felt a little better about being so despondent about my situation last night. If *Cory Miller* couldn't find someone who wanted him for more than swipe-right-one-night, then my only hope probably was, for real, trickster magic.

Fuck. That was a depressing thought.

Right then, Raziel's wings kicked up a breeze as he levitated off the door and gestured wildly out the window. "Oh! Oh! Look! There *is* a Pinkberry here! I told you, Andras! I told you!"

From my left shoulder came a sharp string of colorful curses, followed by, "Please, don't take this wanker in that place. I'll sell you *my* bloody soul if you—"

"Oh, shut up!" Raziel whirled around and shot Andras a glare. "You haven't got a soul to sell!"

"I do so! That's slander, you—"

"Can it, demon." Raziel turned a pleading look on me. "Can we? Please? I love Pinkberry, and it's been *ages!*"

"Bollocks, it has!" Andras groaned. "For the love of—do not take him in there. I'm beggin' ya."

Cory was laughing so hard now, it was a miracle he was keeping my car between the lines.

For my part, I couldn't help chuckling. As much as this whole situation was threatening to break my brain, there was something unavoidably comical about my shoulder angel and demon arguing about whether we should stop for ice cream. "Uh, why shouldn't we take him to Pinkberry?"

Raziel crossed his arms. "Because Andras doesn't think—"

"Because Andras doesn't think anyone needs an angel on a bloody sugar high, that's why." Andras gave a long-suffering sigh and muttered some more curses.

Cory wiped his eyes, still laughing. "Wait, so angels can go on sugar highs? Seriously?"

"They most certainly can *not*," Raziel declared.

"Aye, they can," Andras countered. "And the reports from our last three assignments have got detailed lists of everything that's been damaged as a result."

"Damaged?" I asked. "Sugar high or not, what in the world can a six-inch angel damage?"

"You'd be surprised," Andras grumbled.

Raziel just huffed again and turned to look out the window, arms still crossed. Andras sat down hard on my shoulder and swore again.

And Cory...

Seriously, there was just something about the way this man laughed. The smile. The blush. The crinkles by his dark eyes, which always sparkled when he was overcome with amusement.

Now that I thought about it, hadn't he said he was wary of the Unseelies and all the other tricksters because of his job? Maybe one of them *had* done something to mess with his love life.

I kept that thought to myself, but made a mental note to talk to my paralegal on Monday. I needed to talk to her anyway, since she understood this type of magic—the kind that involved love and relationships—even better than I did. If there was a curse or something out there with Cory's name on it, she'd find it.

For now, we were getting into the Fae District, and the Unseelie Building was coming into view up ahead on the left.

Cory swallowed, eyeing the building. "So you said it's across the street?"

"Yeah." I leaned forward a little, craning my neck. "There. The Public Parking sign after the café."

"The Public—ah. There it is." He put on his signal and

started to slow down.

Inside was a manned ticket booth. Cory opened the window, and the attendant peered into the car. "May I have your license plate number?"

My instinct to jump in and say that he absolutely could *not* have it had me sucking in a breath to speak, but Cory just smiled. "No, you may not."

The man scowled, but he printed out a ticket and handed it to Cory. As Cory pulled away from the booth, I had to smile myself. I should've known he was too savvy to fall for a trickster's attempt to take my license plate number. He'd probably had as many clients as I had who'd received tickets for driving unlicensed vehicles.

"I swear it's registered!" I remembered one particularly incensed client bellowing. "Why would I be driving around with a blank plate?"

"You registered it, and you had a numbered plate," I'd calmly said. "But you gave the number to a fae, didn't you?"

The epiphany, followed by the *oh, fuck my life* sigh was one I'd witnessed many, many times. Cory probably had too.

The fae and all the other tricksters could be frustrating, but they definitely kept life interesting.

I glanced at Raziel. Then at Andras. Then I suppressed a sigh as Cory eased into a parking space. Yeah, the tricksters kept life from getting boring, but man, that could be a double-edged sword sometimes.

Cory set the brake, shut off the engine, and turned to me. "All right. We're here. Shall we?"

I nodded, and as we got out of the car, I hoped like hell we weren't wasting our time.

Because I had no idea what I was going to do if I had to take Andras and Raziel into a courtroom.

CHAPTER 4

CORY

Matt and I walked to a bank of elevators, and he jabbed the call button. As we waited, I glanced at his tiny entourage.

Raziel seemed to prefer to float just above Matt's shoulder, keeping himself in place with gentle motions of his impressive wings. Andras was winged, too, and he could clearly use them, but his default was apparently to park his ass on Matt's shoulder or collarbone. I wondered if Matt could feel the weight of the demon or the movements of the angel's wings. The wings did flutter his hair a little, so... maybe?

But I didn't ask. I was curious about the whole setup, but Matt had bigger things to think about right now.

The elevator opened, and we stepped inside. Matt glared at the buttons, pushed out a resigned breath, and requested the twelfth floor.

As the elevator lurched into motion, I cautiously said, "Not looking forward to this?"

"Not particularly." He tilted his head to one side, then the other, cracking his neck as Raziel darted out of the way and Andras ducked. Either unaware or unfazed, Matt stared up at the numbers above the doors and muttered, "She wasn't my easiest client. I'm not looking forward to being on the other side of the negotiation table."

Whoa. That was... ominous. I didn't get the impression he was intimidated. I doubted there was anyone alive who could intimidate Matt Russo. But I could buy that he didn't think this was going to be pleasant or easy. Never was when you were opposing a trickster. Ask me how I know.

On the twelfth floor, we got out and walked down a bland, corporate hallway. The whole building was bland and corporate, honestly—pastel colors, etched names on windowed doors, block letter directories, potted plants with leaves the size of my thigh, ugly carpet that was somehow simultaneously pink, brown, and gray.

One of my clients theorized that the more chaotic fae— the ones who really loved to cause trouble and screw with people—often worked in environments like this. It looked official and non-threatening. It caused people to let their guards down. I'd long suspected it was true, and that might've been the cause of the hair on my neck standing on end right now. Good thing I didn't have an annoyingly observant angel on my shoulder to point that out to anyone.

At the end of the bland and non-threatening hallway, Matt indicated a door on our left. Two names were etched across the glass: *Rhiannon Mair Cadwallader and Bridget Breathnach.* Below that: *Matchmakers.*

I was pretty sure I'd heard both of those names before from my own clients. That didn't bode well.

I kept that to myself as we walked into their office.

The waiting room was set up like a doctor's office—a high desk, chairs around a coffee table, and a door leading to what I assumed were more rooms beyond. This room had quite a bit more life and character than the rest of the building, though. Some sort of climbing plant had vines rising out of a clay pot and branching across the walls and ceiling, colorful flowers blooming amidst leaves and tendrils. And I didn't think I'd ever seen so many rocks. The coffee table was covered with them, apart from a couple of pamphlet holders and three cork coasters wedged in between geodes, crystals, plain but oddly shaped stones, and a chunk of obsidian. Shelves on the walls held more of the same alongside climbing vines. Somewhere, birds were chirping. I genuinely couldn't tell if they were real or recorded.

The mismatched chairs weren't the most attractive furniture in the world, but they were comfortable. We sat in the nearest two, and steadfastly avoided eye contact with the other two people in the room. There was often a hint of shame among people consulting with fae, and it wasn't unusual to see people wearing hoodies and sunglasses (like the person across from me) or obvious wigs and makeup (like the woman to Matt's left). People really, really didn't want to be seen in a place like this.

The other two clients eyed Matt—or, more likely, Andras and Raziel—but quickly averted their eyes to their phones. They weren't exactly in a position to judge.

Matt exchanged texts with someone. Then he lowered his phone and spoke just loud enough for me to hear, "She said it's going to be a while. She's fitting us in between clients. Sorry."

"Don't apologize to me," I whispered back. "I'm here to help. If it takes a while, it takes a while."

He met my eyes, his brow pinched with a degree of uncertainty I seriously wasn't used to seeing in him. "You probably had plans today."

"Yeah, well, when a friend needs help..." I waved a hand. "That becomes my plans."

His expression turned apologetic. "I owe you."

"Nah, don't worry about that." I nudged his elbow with mine. "I'm not fae. I'm your friend."

He studied me, and a smile slowly came to life. "Still. I'll make it up to you."

I shrugged but said nothing more.

His client wasn't kidding about this taking a while. I'd been to the ends of the internet and back on my phone, and boredom drove me to pick up one of the pamphlets about the matchmaking practice.

I had no idea if we were here to see Bridget or Rhiannon, so I read both their bios. They certainly did break up the boredom, too, because almost without fail, the lives fae led were fascinating.

Over the course of a handful of paragraphs, I'd learned that Bridget was descended from Ireland's Tuatha de Danann, and over the centuries, she'd wandered the earth, endlessly curious about mortals. With time, she'd begun to understand how love and relationships worked, and she'd helped guide countless mortals to love. She claimed to be responsible for an impressive list of famous lovers, from Richard II and Anne of Bohemia to Lauren Bacall and Humphrey Bogart.

Christ. Next to this, my Linkedin was looking about as dull as the pink-brown-gray carpet in the hallway outside.

I turned over the pamphlet, and Rhiannon's profile made Bridget's look as dull as mine. She was of the Gwragedd Annwn from a Welsh lake called Llyn Barfog. Like many lake maidens, she'd married a mortal man at some point. The Gwragedd Annwn were well known for leaving men who crossed them, especially those who used violence, but Rhiannon had instead taken vengeance on her husband. First she'd convinced the Bwbachod the house goblins—to make his life miserable. Then, when he'd decided to flee to another town, she'd enlisted the Gwyllion in the mountains to lure him off his path and get him lost in the woods. He was never seen or heard from again.

Since then, she'd made it her mission to help scorned and mistreated women out of their relationships, and over time, that had expanded to helping people of all genders find their way *into* healthier unions. And if a partner turned toxic or abusive... Well, she was still more than happy to help with that.

I skimmed over the text again. Why did I have a feeling we were here to see Rhiannon? Because a matchmaker who also moonlighted in terrorizing and disappearing abusers seemed like someone who'd need a lawyer from time to time.

And now that I thought about it... maybe she had room in her client list? Because as much as I didn't want to tangle with the fae—especially not a Welsh lake maiden turned vigilante—desperate times called for desperate measures.

I glanced at Matt.

At the demon fidgeting on his shoulder and being loudly bored by way of harsh sighs and the odd "bloody hell."

Okay, maybe I didn't need to be hiring the fae. Not for this. Not for anything.

A solid ninety minutes after we'd arrived in this waiting room—long enough I was pretty sure one of the vines had actually stretched a few inches closer to one of the shelves—Matt's phone pinged.

He checked it, then rose. "That's her. Let's go."

My heart started pounding as I followed him into the back. This was it. If she wouldn't help Matt, then... Well, then I had no idea what Plan B was.

He pushed open the door, which led us into a hallway with four doors on either side. Another plant like the one in the waiting room stood in a huge black pot, its vines stretching up the walls, across the ceiling, down the opposite walls. Flowers and leaves hung low enough that Matt had to duck his head slightly to avoid them. I'm a little shorter than him, so I didn't need to duck, but I did anyway just out of an irrational certainty one of the vines would try to grab me. What could I say? I'd spent enough time around tricksters to be wary of everything in their spaces. Even Raziel and Andras seemed to give the dangling plants a wide berth, so maybe it wasn't so irrational after all.

At the third door on the left, Matt halted. He put his hand up to knock, but paused, closed his eyes, and worked his jaw for a few seconds. Then he pushed a breath out through his nose, opened his eyes, and knocked sharply.

The door swung inward. Matt and I trooped inside, and—

Whoa. This wasn't what I'd expected.

While the rest of the suite was dripping in plant life, this office was jarringly sterile and monochrome. Every surface—a desk, a file cabinet, and two shelves—was gleaming white. Two books stood on one of the shelves. A Bonsai tree sat on the file cabinet. The desk was bare apart from a single fountain pen beside a leatherbound book and a white, steaming mug on a black coaster.

And behind the desk, dressed in a sharp, black pantsuit, sat a dark-eyed white woman with freckles across her nose and startlingly copper hair tumbling over her shoulders. The corners of her mouth rose slightly, hovering in that space between a smile and a smirk.

Matt gazed down at her. Voice taut, he gritted out, "Bridget."

She dipped her chin slightly as her ambiguous expression shifted to a more distinct smile. "Mr. Russo." Her eyes flicked to, I assumed, the angel and demon. "Raziel. Andras."

"Hello, ma'am," Raziel chirped with way too much cheer.

Andras just grumbled something in the ballpark of a greeting.

Her intense eyes shifted to me, and I couldn't help standing a bit straighter. She pursed her lips as she studied me, but after a beat or two, the smile returned. "You must be Mr. Russo's neighbor."

Matt and I both jumped.

"Huh?" I asked.

He cocked his head. "How... How do you know who he is?"

The smile came fully to life but didn't exactly add any warmth to her expression. "I know a lot of things. Now." She gestured at the pair of stark white chairs in front of her desk. "Why don't you have a seat so we can get down to business?"

Matt and I exchanged glances. Then we both sat. I couldn't say the hard, weirdly angled chair was particularly comfortable, but it was probably the least of our concerns right now.

Andras sat on Matt's shoulder, this time with his hands behind him and his head lolling to one side, looking for all the world like a kid who was bored senseless. Why was it so tempting to reach over and knock him off? Probably because he seemed to think this was all just an inconvenience and no big deal. Meanwhile my Saturday had been thrown off the rails. And that was to say nothing of how this was all affecting Matt.

"So." Bridget sat up and folded her long fingers on her bright white desk. Even her nails were painted white. "What can I do for you, Mr. Russo?"

"I need to do something about"—Matt gestured at each of his shoulders—"*them.*"

Nodding slowly, she spoke with what sounded like exaggerated concern, "I see." Then she flipped open her leather book, revealing what appeared to be a ledger. After leafing through a few pages, she stopped on one and ran her finger down to a particular line. "Well, this is what we agreed to, yes?" She met his gaze across the desk again. "You wanted my help finding a companion."

Matt's cheeks colored, and he sighed as he rolled his eyes. "How exactly are they going to help me find someone?"

"By guiding you, of course." She folded her hands on the pages again. "They're both very, very good at what they do."

My neck prickled. I'd worked around the fae far too long not to be suspicious of everything they said or did. Every bit of subtext they could tuck into body language, expressions, and intonation. I had no idea what her angle was, only that I could see—could *feel*—that trickster spark in her eyes.

Even more than the temptation to knock Andras off Matt's shoulder, the temptation was almost irresistible to nudge Matt's foot with mine, or to find a way to interrupt this meeting, or... *something.* Anything to hit the pause button and get a sidebar with him. I had to warn him that—

"I'm not interested in playing games, Bridget," he said coolly. "The whole point is to find a companion or get laid or... whatever." Matt waved a hand. "But that isn't going to happen when I have *them.*"

Bridget gave one of those weird trickster smiles that said she was absolutely up to something. "Well, you'll have them to guide you. That's what they're there for."

"Right, and they kind of defeat the purpose when any man who looks my way is going to turn tail and run *because* of them."

I half-expected Andras and Raziel to get offended by that, but Andras shrugged as if, yeah, he got it. Raziel said something that sounded like "He's got a point." This apparently wasn't their first rodeo, after all.

Bridget's features hardened, and she touched her chest. "Mr. Russo. Are you telling me I don't know how to do my job?"

Oh, fuck. Danger. Danger! Don't insult the fae, Matt!

Matt's expression stayed neutral, though his voice took on a sharper edge. "I'm saying that I have unique circumstances that warrant further negotiation to make sure this agreement is truly beneficial to me."

My heart pounded. He was treading on dangerous ground without flinching. Completely cool and confident.

Holy shit, that's hot.

Bridget glared at Matt. "And what unique circumstances are those?"

He glared right back. "Well, as you pointed out during our conversation last night, I'm a successful attorney. That's something a partner would find attractive, is it not?"

Oh, the look on her face now—as if she already knew she were cornered by her own words—so dangerous, and yet so satisfying. I had to fight hard not to squirm in my chair, especially since it would probably squeak and give me away.

Bridget exhaled through her nose. "A partner would certainly—"

"Yes or no, Bridget." Ice on his words. A little shiver went up my spine, but it wasn't that usual dread I got in a fae's crosshairs. No, this was something else entirely. I couldn't tear my gaze away from Matt as he stared down the trickster. Maybe it was because she was a client, or maybe it was because she was trying to put Matt's balls in a vise, but this conversation was bringing out the bulldog lawyer in him, and... Jesus, the frisson it gave me to watch him in action.

Oblivious to me trying not to drool, Bridget pressed her lips into a thin line so bleached it nearly matched her office décor. "Aye. Yes."

"Right." Matt nodded sharply. "So you understand that jeopardizing my career will make me less desirable, and will therefore make it more difficult for me to find a mate. Correct?"

She narrowed her eyes. "It would—"

"Yes or no," he snapped.

The way her jaw worked, it was a wonder I didn't hear her teeth grinding. A mix of fear and excitement swirled in my stomach. He was playing with fire, cross examining a fae like this, but he was also sexy as hell while he did it. Be still my heart.

Bridget sat back in her chair, crossing her arms. Drumming her white-painted nails on her upper arm, she gritted out, "Aye."

"And as you've admitted under oath at least twice in my presence, you are well aware of the stigma associated with demonstrable use of magic for personal or professional gains. Correct?"

She gave a reluctant nod.

Matt smiled the smile of a chess player who'd just moved his opponent into checkmate. "So we agree there's..." He gestured at Andras and Raziel. "A problem?"

I would never in a million years want to be in the crosshairs of a fae who was snared in her own trap, but watching Matt navigate this was... fuuuck.

Her voice was frosty as she asked, "What is it you want, Mr. Russo?" Some of that trickster spark came back to her narrowed eyes, and one corner of her mouth rose as she added, "Would you like to be released from our agreement? Because, as I've also said under oath in your presence, the fae take it as a grave insult when someone backs out of such an agreement."

The only hint that she'd found a chink in his armor was his hard swallow, but he rallied quickly. "I'd like to *amend* our agreement." He smiled. "You know, clarify a few things and compromise on a few details so that it's as fair and mutually beneficial as I know the fae prefer."

I almost whistled at the brass balls it took to say that to her face. Would the sudden red in her cheeks be that obvious if she hadn't been against such a bright white backdrop? No idea, but she was clearly not pleased.

"Fine," she said through her teeth. "What part would you like to amend?"

"For starters, I need them gone during working hours." He thumped his knuckle on the table. "*Gone*. Full stop."

She pursed her lips.

"If they're visible when I'm at work, *especially* when I'm in court," he went on, "then there's a damn good chance I'll lose my job. And my reputation." Matt cocked a brow. "So who will you call next time a client wants to sue you?"

Oh, she was not pleased. "Is that all?"

"No." He leaned back and folded his hands in his lap, affecting boredom, which had to be a deliberate means of antagonizing her. "I need them gone when I'm actually on the prowl. If I'm meeting someone, if I'm at a club, if I'm FaceTiming with someone..." He half-shrugged, nearly sending Andras tumbling. "That has to be me and only me."

Her thin-lipped scowl turned to a sneer. "And being a savvy attorney, I'm sure you'd never exploit a loophole by claiming you're *always* on the prowl, and therefore they need to be gone all the time."

His chuckle wasn't a denial.

As they stared each other down, I still had to fight the urge to squirm. Admittedly, Bridget intimidated me. She clearly didn't have that effect on Matt, though, and his cool brazenness had my pulse pounding for reasons that had nothing to do with being in the presence of a pissed-off fae.

"You wanted this, Mr. Russo," Bridget said flatly. "You asked me to help you find a companion. And if you recall, that's exactly what I do." She inclined her head. "So I know what I'm doing, yes?"

"You know what—"

"Yes or no, Mr. Russo," she snapped.

He tightened his jaw. "Yes."

"Right." Her smile returned, frosty as ever. "Then perhaps you should defer to my expertise, hmm? I know what I'm doing."

"You do," he said. "But I'm also correct that, as it stands, your methods are going to ruin my chances with anyone, and quite possibly ruin my *life*. So I don't think I'm out of line asking for some modifications."

They glared across the desk again.

After a moment, Matt said, "Look, we both know you're going to end up in my office again sooner or later. Because everyone in the fae district needs an attorney sometimes, and I'm the *last* attorney in this city who'll give *you* the time of day."

The subtle tightness of her lips told me he wasn't wrong.

Matt continued, "So, in the interest of maintaining a mutually beneficial relationship going forward, I don't think I'm out of line here."

"Perhaps not. But don't think you can come in here and try to play games and exploit a loophole to—"

"No, no, I wouldn't dream of it." He showed his palms. "That's how tricksters do things, not lawyers."

She actually rolled her eyes.

"Oh, for fuck's sake," Andras piped up, still lounging on Matt's shoulder like a bored kindergartener. "The sooner you wankers sort out this bollocks, the sooner Raziel and me can finish this assignment." He pushed himself to his feet, snapped his wings once, and crossed his arms. "He wants us gone when he's at work or on the prowl, fine. She wants us still there enough to do our job, great. Now can we get on with it already? We're already hours into this and ain't done a bloody thing except listen to whinging and bickering." He paused, rolling his eyes. "Well, and listen to that one lose his bloody mind over Pinkberry."

That last part actually got a laugh out of both Bridget and Matt.

From Matt's other shoulder, Raziel made a haughty sound and grumbled, "You love Pinkberry too."

Matt was fighting a losing battle against his amusement, but he managed to school his expression—sort of—enough to say, "He makes a valid point."

Bridget's eyebrow shot up. "About Pinkberry?"

"Well, you have to admit," I interjected timidly. "It is pretty good."

Matt quirked his lips. Then he sighed. "Goddammit. Now I want Pinkberry." He sat up. "Fine. Let's iron this out and then get out of here before I end up with a hangry angel on my shoulder."

"Hangry?" Raziel asked. "What's that?"

Andras cackled. "It's you when you haven't eaten." He prodded Matt's earlobe with his pointy tail. "Hurry up. You don't want to see that."

Matt slid his gaze toward me, an adorable grin on his lips. "I... kind of do, actually."

"No," Bridget and Andras said in unison. "You don't."

Matt straightened. "Well, then." He cleared his throat. "Let's get a move on."

There had been a handful of occasions in our five-year friendship where I'd witnessed Matt turning on the Matthew A. Russo, Esquire, and every one of them had left my heart going wild.

Like the time we'd been visiting a former neighbor who'd told us her new landlord was neglecting repairs on her apartment. Matt had gotten on the phone with the guy and given it to him with both barrels, quoting state and municipal law off the top of his head and threatening to represent the nice old lady pro bono if he didn't get his shit together. By the time that conversation had been over, Mrs. Tanner was getting a refund on two months' rent, the landlord was putting in emergency calls to a plumber and electrician, and I'd been so turned on I couldn't see straight.

Today, as I drove us out of the Fae District, I was jittery and restless, my palms sweaty on the wheel as I begged my dick not to pitch an unwelcome tent. Matt was so distracted

he probably wouldn't have noticed, but Andras would probably have pointed it out just to be an asshole.

Though he was somewhat distracted at the moment.
Like Raziel, he was poring over the amended agreement
with Matt. As the three of them bickered about exactly
what the new clause meant, I followed the GPS's directions
toward the Pinkberry Raziel had spotted earlier. I generally
tried to stick to the speed limit, but admittedly, I was
pushing it a bit right now. Partly to avoid a hangry angel—
though it might've been too late, given the snappy
comments he was exchanging with Matt and Andras—and
partly so I could get out of this damn car and catch my
breath. I needed to think, damn it, and I couldn't do that
while I was sitting beside Matt.

Why was I so stupid? Matt was miles out of my league.
If there was any hope of him noticing me, wouldn't one of
his celestial pests have gestured at me by now and said, *"Oh,
hey, have you thought about hooking up with* this *fine male
specimen?"*

Well, apart from Raziel's comment earlier, which Matt
had shot down. But Bridget hadn't suggested it, so...

I mean, matchmaking was what they all did. It was what
Bridget did. The consensus among the three of them was
clearly that Mr. Right had not been in Bridget's office, so...
yeah. I was out of luck.

Damn. I was happy to help Matt with this as much as I
could, but... not gonna lie—it was a gut punch. What I
wouldn't have done to turn Matt's head.

Though, maybe I wouldn't enlist a trickster's help. That
never seemed like a good idea, and after today, I was even
less inclined to enter into an agreement with one. Knowing
my luck, I'd probably end up turned into a deer or a donkey
or something. Or otherwise tangled up in a way that would

require me to cash in that favor I had on reserve from Galen the Trickster King.

I glanced at Matt, who was still engaged in a loud debate with Andras about... something. Raziel sounded pissed off too. Hangry angels—what can you do?

Facing the road again, I debated letting Matt have my favor from the Trickster King. Because if anyone could get someone out from under this fae deal, it was Galen.

Then again, maybe it would work out. Maybe, somehow, Andras and Raziel would find Matt the partner he so desperately wanted.

So... no. I'd hold on to my favor. Maybe save it until I was the one desperate for a partner. Which I was.

Ugh. I need to spend some more time on Grindr, dammit.

CHAPTER 5

MATT

I was exhausted. Holy shit.

We hadn't even been in Bridget's office all that long, and negotiating the specifics of a contract was something I did every day. The task was nothing compared to some of the meetings, depositions, and trials that were routine parts of my job. Still, I felt like I'd just endured a grueling court-room trial followed by hours of unrelated depositions and a masochistically over-the-top workout at the gym.

Probably because there'd been so much at stake this time. It wasn't the physical or mental exhaustion that came from a long day—it was pure stress.

Sagging back on my couch, I rubbed my eyes with my thumb and forefinger. Fuck me. What a day. And it wasn't even noon yet.

It didn't help that Andras had been correct about two things: hangry Raziel, and sugar-high Raziel. The former had been appeased by a thimble-sized portion of pome-granate frozen yogurt. The latter... oh my God.

"First things first, let's zhuzh up your profiles." His wing whipped my ear as he flailed around beside my head. "Let's see what you've got. Come on. Laptop out." He clapped his hands. "What are you waiting for?"

"A laptop?" Andras barked a laugh. "D'you even know what decade this is?" He nudged my shoulder with his foot. "Get out your mobile."

I groaned, and what could I do but dig out my phone? The sooner they did what they came to do, the sooner they'd be gone.

"And if they haven't succeeded within thirty days," Bridget's voice echoed in my ears, *"then the agreement reverts back to the original version."*

No pressure, right?

But she'd argued that if they hadn't been able to complete their task within a month, then either they'd failed or I'd refused to cooperate. The logical response was then to either punish them or revert to 1.0. As annoyed as I was with these two winged dumbasses, I couldn't bring myself to agree to let them be punished for failing to hook me up with someone. I mean, apart from a handful of brief relationships, I hadn't been able to pull it off in the seven years since my divorce. Was it really fair for them to take the heat if they couldn't work an actual miracle in thirty days?

So... fine. We had a month to get me on the radar of a man who thought I was worth a damn. Because the odds of pulling *that* off weren't depressingly grim.

Raziel fluttered forward, probably to get a better look at my screen. "And which dating apps do you have?"

Andras joined him, and he snorted. "Those aren't dating apps. Those are hookup apps."

"Do you know how many people have met their spouses on Tinder?" I tapped the app in question. "Sometimes it starts there."

Raziel made one of those affronted sounds he often did. "That's no way to start a relationship."

I was about to remind him that the whole point of this was to get me laid, and Tinder and Grindr were perfectly good for that, but Andras groaned, "Razi. Can we not do this again? Some people start there."

"But then they're just..." Raziel waved his arms around like one of those inflatables that car dealerships used for some reason. "That's just lust! You can't find love if you're looking for—"

"The fuck he can't!" Andras threw back, and he whipped his tail at Raziel, knocking a yelp out of the angel. To me, he said, "Let's see your profile."

Why was I so embarrassed at the prospect of showing them my Tinder profile? Or—God help me—my Grindr profile? I put those out there specifically for people to see and hopefully connect with me. Made sense to show them to this pair.

Except something told me they'd take one look at them and declare, *"Welp, there's the problem. Your profile is trash, and—well, hell, so are you."*

I rolled my eyes and tapped a profile, but right then, my front door swung open.

"Hey." Cory shot me a smile as he came in with some takeout bags hanging from his wrist. "Sorry. That took longer than I thought it would."

"That's fine." I took in a deep breath through my nose. "Oh, God, that smells good." I put my phone aside, ignoring the protests from Andras and Raziel. "Were they busy?"

Cory actually blushed as he toed off his shoes. "Uh... Well..."

I studied him. "What?"

The blush deepened. "That cute cashier was working

tonight." He gave me an apologetic shrug and a sheepish grin. "I... might've been flirting a bit."

The surge of jealousy almost made me waver on my feet. Only years of practice keeping a poker face in the courtroom and at the deposition table stopped me from letting that jealousy show. Instead, I managed to chuckle as I offered to take the bags. "Yeah? How'd that go?"

Cory handed over the bags, and as we headed for the kitchen, he said, "I mean, he told me I was his favorite customer, and he gave me a free order of breadsticks, so... I guess it went okay?"

I glanced at him, forcing a smile. "Didn't get his number?"

Cory laughed, dropping his gaze as his cheeks turned even redder. "I... I mean... He's at work, you know?" He slid his hands into his pockets and met my gaze through those long lashes. "I didn't want to put him on the spot."

"That's fair." And why was I so relieved? I didn't have a chance in hell with Cory. He quite clearly wasn't into me. So if he connected with someone else, that was a good thing. Wasn't it?

It was, but I was pretty sure I'd die inside the moment I realized he'd locked a man down.

Damn. Forget thirty days. I needed Andras and Raziel to find me a partner *stat* so I wouldn't lose my mind when Cory met someone.

The pair of shoulder pests were still full from Pinkberry, so they didn't partake. Cory and I divided the food between us, including the extra breadsticks the cute cashier had given him. As a means of flirting.

Ugh. God. I wasn't even hungry anymore, but I dug into my food anyway. Cory had picked up some lunch portion pasta dishes from the Italian café across the street from our building. They made some of the best pasta in town, and they didn't cost an arm and a leg. Plus they were close enough we didn't have to bother with delivery apps and all their shady fees.

And Cory can flirt with the—

Matt. Stop. Jesus.

We sat on the couch with our containers and a couple of beers, and I'd barely taken my first bite before Raziel cheerfully announced, "Oh, I have a brilliant idea!"

"Oh, *great*," Andras drawled, letting the sarcasm drip. "*This* should be good."

"Will you just—" Raziel huffed. "Anyhow. Matthew, why don't *you* go flirt with the cashier?"

Both Cory and I choked on our food.

"What?" I sputtered. "Flirt with—are you serious?"

Cory had to put his container down on the coffee table, and he took a swig of beer in between coughing.

"I'm..." I shook my head. "I'm not going to cockblock my friend."

"Cockblock?" Raziel asked, truly confused.

"For fuck's sake!" Andras flew forward a bit, probably so he could glare at Raziel, and he sounded beyond exasperated: "Ya really don't read the briefings, do you?"

"I do!" Raziel snapped.

And... off they went. Arguing. Again.

"Oh my God," I groaned, covering my face with one hand. "Will you two—enough!"

They both shut up, and I realized Cory had jumped. Shit, maybe I'd said that louder than I'd intended.

I exhaled. "Sorry," I said to Cory. He shrugged and continued eating. To Andras and Raziel, I said, "Look, I'm not going to go after someone Cory wants. That would—it's not cool, okay?"

I had no idea if they understood why it wasn't—if that was included in the "briefings" Raziel apparently didn't read—but they let it go.

"All right." I gestured at the coffee table. "Can you two, like, sit there for a bit? I'm going to give myself a headache trying to look at you." That, and just having them moving around right at the edges of my peripheral vision was... weird. With them in front of me and less annoying—sort of —I jabbed a fork into some of penne in my container as I said, "Now. What exactly is the... plan, I guess?"

Andras, who'd sat on the edge of the table with his legs dangling, peered up at Raziel. Raziel looked down at him and shrugged. They had one of those exchanges only two people—or, well, beings—who'd known each other forever could, where an entire conversation was tucked into expressions and gestures.

Finally, Andras rolled his eyes, sighed, and shifted his attention up to me. "Well, obviously you suck at finding a man."

I blinked. Beside me, Cory wheezed with laugher, and when I cut my eyes toward him, he tried valiantly to school his expression. I flipped him off, and he snickered. "Dick."

"What?" he said through his laughter. "Act like you've never been that blunt before."

I shot him a glare, but his smug *am-I-wrong?* smirk just made me laugh, and I shook my head. To Andras, I said, "Okay. Fine. So I'm... not great at connecting with people." I poked at my food with my fork. "And you two are?"

"We excel at guiding people," Raziel said.

"Right," Cory said, "but what about making those connections yourself? Or is this one of those, 'people who can't, teach' things?"

Raziel cocked his head, and I was genuinely surprised

an actual question mark didn't appear above his puzzled face.

Andras sighed. "It's an expression, Razi. Just—" He looked up at us. "No, we don't have partners, but we've been working for Bridget for centuries. We know what the hell we're doing." He paused, then added with a smug look that rivaled Cory's: "More than you do, evidently."

I sat back, exhaling in defeat. "You know what? Fuck you all."

"Oh, come on." Cory nudged my foot with his. "You love it."

I once again tried to shoot him a look. He met me with a smile that somehow toed the line between snarky and fond. Yeah, he was being a little shit just like he often did, but there was no heat behind any of it.

There was some heat of an entirely different variety in me, though. God, what I wouldn't have given to be able to connect with him the way I hadn't been able to connect with anyone else, and not just because that would mean Andras and Raziel were gone.

Do you have any idea how bad I want you?

I pulled my gaze away from him and returned it to the winged matchmakers on the coffee table. "So we've established you guys are better at this than I am. Fine. Now what? What exactly do you do?"

Raziel stood straighter, pushing his shoulders back. "Quite simply, we offer guidance while—"

"We cut out all the bullshit on your profiles," Andras broke in. "We rewrite all of it so you sound like a halfway desirable partner, and then we help you figure out how to actually be that halfway desirable partner."

I stared at him. Then I turned to Cory. "Am I really that blunt with people?"

He was chewing a bite of pasta, and he nodded as he shrugged apologetically.

"Great." To the demon, I said, "So... like you tell me what to say? What to do?"

"And we'll help you pick out a wardrobe!" Raziel sounded positively gleeful, and he clapped his hands as he asked, "Are you ready to go shopping?"

My jaw went slack. "Whoa, whoa, wait." I gestured at them with my fork. "The new agreement says you guys disappear when I'm out in public."

"Well, yes." The angel shrugged. "But you can summon us any time you need us. Like when you're in a dressing room and need someone to approve what you're trying on."

Oh. God. The prospect of listening to these two heckle my clothing choices in between arguing with each other sounded... uh... delightful.

Cory cleared his throat. "I, um... I can go with you, too."

I faced him. "Huh?"

"I like shopping for clothes. And you *have* told me I have good taste." He shrugged as he spun some more noodles on his fork. "If you want, I can help."

Why did my heart go wild at thought of taking him with me? And at the same time, my stomach knotted, because I didn't want his help picking out clothes to date other men. I wanted his help picking out clothes to date *him*.

But the first option was the best I was going to get, so I nodded. "Sure. Yeah." I managed a smile. "That would be great."

His face lit up as if he were actually excited about this.

And suddenly... I was too.

CHAPTER 6

CORY

After we'd eaten, Matt collected our food containers and tossed them. Then he came back to the couch and eyed Andras and Raziel warily. "So... I guess we should get back to my profiles?" He glanced at me. "We were about to start that earlier when you brought the food."

"Ooh, so I didn't miss it." I chuckled and slid closer to him as he got out his phone. I'd only meant to move in enough that I could see his screen, but...

Fuck. Sitting this close to him... while we were talking about finding a man for him...

It seemed fitting there was a demon in the room, because I was pretty sure this was actual Hell.

At least Andras had moved from the coffee table to perching in the crook of Matt's elbow. Still weird as hell, but better than having him right next to my head.

Matt pulled up one of several hookup/dating apps on his phone and opened his profile. Raziel flew in closer, and Andras craned his neck to read it.

Then Andras sat back, snapping his wings like he did whenever he was annoyed. "Well, no wonder you can't get your arse fucked." He gestured wildly at the screen. "What d'you expect, you numpty?"

Matt gave him one of those sharp looks that I imagined made opposing counsel squirm in their chairs in the courtroom. It made me want to squirm, too, but not because I was intimidated or nervous.

Is it hot in here? Fuuuck.

Andras, of course, didn't even flinch, staring back with more defiance than a creature that tiny should've been able to muster. "Well? Why would any man be arsed to respond to... *that?*" He pointed at the screen again.

Matt glared harder. Andras glared more defiantly.

Raziel cleared his throat. "For starters, perhaps we could make your introduction a little more... inviting?"

That broke the standoff, and Raziel drew all our attention to the phone. I wasn't sure when the angel had conjured the pointer, but he gestured at the screen like a teacher.

"Perhaps something less confrontational?" He glanced up at Matt. "Not so negative?"

"No, no." Andras shook his head. "There ain't a thing wrong with telling people upfront what he doesn't like. Then he isn't wasting their bloody time. No, the problem is *this.*" He flew closer, snatched the pointer from Raziel, and whacked it against the screen so hard I was surprised he didn't crack the glass. "D'you really think *this* is attractive, man?"

I craned my neck a little to read the text, pretending not to notice that my shoulder was now pressed up against Matt's. Raziel had indicated the problem was in the lines, *"Not interested in guys half my age, and my time is very limited. Let's not waste it, shall we?"*

Andras took exception to *"Looking for love, but this vers bottom won't say no to a hookup."*

Whew. Yeah. Matt did need some help in this department. It wasn't terrible, especially the part Andras was throwing a fit over, but it could probably be a little less cheesy and a little more tactful.

And thanks, guys. Thanks for making sure I now know my hot neighbor likes to bottom. That'll help me hold on to my sanity. Thanks a lot.

I was going to shrivel up and die before this conversation was over, either from embarrassment, unrequited horniness, or both.

Mercifully unaware of me losing my damn mind beside him, Matt exhaled. "So, what should I put instead?"

Both celestial assistants started to speak, but I beat them to the punch. "Why don't you let me take a crack at it?" I held out my hand. "See if I can write something that works better?"

Matt turned to me. "You... You think you can?"

"Oh, honey." I plucked the phone from between his hands. "I'm pretty sure I can come up with something better than this."

He stared at me for a moment, then nodded. "Okay. Sure. I'm terrible at these, so..."

In unison, Andras, Raziel, and I said, "You are."

His exasperated groan was hilarious and adorable. "Fuck all of you."

I opened up the editing option and erased the godawful text that was already there. I started typing, but paused. "How, uh, how forward do you want this to be? I know it says you're cool with hookups"—why was my face burning?—"but is that still what you want? Or do you want to focus on something more serious?"

Matt blushed too, and he half-shrugged. "I'm good with hookups. And if I'm dating someone, I kind of like to get the sexual compatibility out of the way before we waste too much time, you know?"

Raziel threw up his hands. "Good heavens. No wonder you're still single! You're supposed to meet people and—"

"Razi." Andras sighed as he flew back to his perch in the crook of Matt's elbow. "It's the Twenty-first century. People hook up. Make peace with it already."

From the disgruntled noise the angel made, he had no intention of making peace with it.

I chuckled, then cleared my throat. "Okay. Got it." I started typing, calling on everything I'd ever put into my profiles, not to mention what drew my attention to other guys. Then again, I'd had a horrible string of bad luck with men, so maybe it wasn't such a hot idea to model Matt's profile after mine or theirs.

While I dealt with that, Raziel chirped, "What about photos? Because those"—he flapped a wing toward the phone in my hand—"aren't going to work."

Matt sighed as if this were exhausting him. It probably was. "What's wrong with my photos?"

At the same time Raziel declared, "You need professional photos!", Andras said, "Too many fecking clothes!"

I looked up from the screen. Matt's exasperated, annoyed, and vaguely amused expression was hilarious. And... maybe a little attractive.

"So, what?" He let the sarcasm drip. "Should I get kill two birds with one stone and get professional nudes?"

Andras's shrug suggested he thought that was the perfect solution.

Raziel, of course, tsked. "No. They don't need to be

nudes. But, yes, perhaps some professional photos? Oh! Maybe *after* we've fixed up your wardrobe."

Matt watched them for a moment. Then he swung his gaze to me. "I swear to God, if this takes more than a few days, bro code be damned—I'm moving in on that cashier just to get these two out of here."

I kicked him. "Don't you dare. I've got dibs."

His expression turned plaintive. "And I've got... *them.*"

I just laughed and continued with his profile. After a minute or so, I handed back his phone, not sure why I suddenly had a ball of anxiety in the pit of my stomach. Because he might hate what I'd written? Or because it might work and summon Mr. Perfect right to Matt's door?

Matt furrowed his brow as he read the screen.

"Well?" Raziel demanded. "What does it say?"

Matt rolled his eyes. Then he read aloud, "'I'm a busy professional in my 40s. Hit me up and tell me about yourself. Looking for love, but not opposed to having a good time if the chemistry is there. I'm a pretty low-key guy who enjoys a low-key life. I like to be active, I like to relax—just depends on the mood. Looking for someone to enjoy both of those things and everything in between. I know my way around the kitchen—let me cook you my enchiladas, and you'll love me forever! LOL. My time is limited, but I'll make time for you.'"

He stared at the phone. Then he turned to me, eyes wide. "That... Shit." He faced the phone again, and he sounded incredulous. "I should've had you write something for me ages ago."

I laughed softly, pretending my heart didn't ache at the prospect of other men falling all over themselves to message him now.

"It's much better," Raziel said with a sharp nod.

Andras apparently disagreed, if the gagging sound he made was any indication.

"What?" Matt demanded.

"Nothing?" Andras shrugged flippantly. "Just... all that's gonna get you is more wankers and tadgers."

"It will not!" Raziel declared. "I think it sounds nice." To me, he said, "Well done, Cory."

Andras mimicked, "Well done, Cory."

Matt narrowed his eyes at the demon. "So help me, I will get a flyswatter."

Andras barked a laugh. "You think a flyswatter's gonna hurt me? Pfft."

"An electric one might," I said.

Matt turned to me, eyebrows up. "Do you have one of those?"

"No, but I could probably Amazon Prime it." I took out my phone and pulled up the app. "Or maybe a stun gun?"

"Oi!" The demon flailed around, his wings whipping up a small but violent wind. "You'd better not!"

"Or what?" Matt asked dryly. "You'll slap me with your wing? *Again?*"

Andras huffed. Then he smacked the side of Matt's wrist with his tail.

"Ow!" Matt slapped at his arm, knocking Andras away in the process.

The demon squawked, caught the edge of Matt's sleeve, and righted himself.

"Huh." I pursed my lips. "Maybe the regular flyswatter will work after all."

"Eh." Matt nodded at my phone. "Get the electric one just in case. I'm keeping these two in line by any means necessary."

"I beg your pardon!" Raziel hmphed. "I believe you mean keeping *that one* in line!"

"Nope." Matt focused on his own screen. "Both of you."

That prompted some grumbling, but otherwise, the pair settled down. When I glanced at Matt, I wasn't at all surprised to see him fighting a smile. Nor was I surprised by the rush of heat that impish look sent through me.

I am such a dumbass for you. My God.

I was also glad to see Matt's sense of humor seemed to have returned. He was still stressed about all this, I was sure, but he could snark with me and at the winged idiots. He could laugh. So... that was promising. Meant he was out of panic mode, at least.

We went through the rest of his profile, filling in some of his interests in more detail. Favorite movies, TV shows he enjoyed, if he had kids or pets (or wanted them in the future).

It was... excruciating.

I already knew Matt was a walking list of everything I wanted in a man, but carefully cataloguing it all and phrasing it to appeal to every male-attracted man in the city except for me—that stung. Every time he rattled off another detail about what he wanted in a partner and in a relationship, I wanted to toss his phone across the room—or at his stupid head—and shout, *"I'm right here, Matt!"*

But... no. I just dutifully helped him put it out there that he didn't like movies for first dates because even if it gave them something to talk about afterward, it meant three hours of disengaging from each other. I spelled out that he wanted kids someday and longed for a place where he could finally have a dog again. I typed out for other men to see that one of Matt's favorite things in the world was laughing and joking in the kitchen while he prepared a meal together with someone, as if that wasn't one of *my* favorite things to do *with Matt*.

By the end of it, I was a wreck, but I kept it to myself. Matt wanted what he wanted, and what he wanted wasn't me. That was just how it was.

Ugh. This sucked. Was that cashier's shift over? Maybe I could catch him as he was leaving and see if he wanted to grab a cup of coffee and...

And then I'd probably unload all my frustration on him and turn him off forever, because all I'd be thinking about was the legions of men who were going to find Matt's shiny new profile. I might as well have included the text *"I'm basically interested in anyone but you, Cory."* Fuck.

After Matt had activated the last updated profile, I sat up and picked up my own phone. Surreptitiously putting some space between us on his couch, I said, "It's, um... I should probably get out of your hair." I gestured with my phone. "It's almost five, and I still need to get a few things done today."

Matt seemed startled by that, but he recovered quickly and nodded. "Sure. Yeah." He rose. "Thanks again for... God, for everything. I'm pretty sure I'd have lost my mind today without your help."

And I'm losing my mind today with you, so... yay?

But I forced a smile. "Any time. You know that."

His smile was everything. "I owe you. And, um..." He suddenly seemed shy and uncertain. "You're really on for shopping? And..." He shot a glance at Raziel, rolled his eyes, and added, "And maybe helping us do some photos after?"

I died inside all over again. "Of course. Do you have time tomorrow?" *Let's get this shit over with.* "I've got the whole day free."

He chewed his lip as his eyes lost focus. Then he

nodded. "Yeah. Tomorrow would be great." He smiled again. "I'll buy lunch. And... probably dinner, since I doubt this will be a quick process with them around."

"Sounds good. Text me when you want to head out. I'll be up."

We said our goodbyes, and I left his apartment like it was on fire. Fortunately, my own place was downstairs, because with as pathetic and worn out as I was right then, I didn't see me dragging myself up two flights of stairs.

I keyed myself in, shut the door, and leaned against it. Eyes closed, I pushed out a long breath through my nose.

I wanted Matt to be happy. I wanted him to find love. He deserved all that and more. But oh, God, this was killing me.

Because someone in this city was about to hit the jackpot.

And it wasn't going to be me.

CHAPTER 7

MATT & CORY

Matt

Despite the noisy, irritating presence of Andras and Raziel, my apartment was startlingly empty and quiet after Cory left. I stretched out on my couch, which suddenly felt too big without Cory right beside me, and I kept thumbing through my newly revised profiles in search of things I should tweak. It was something to do. Without that to hold my attention, I was restless in a way I didn't fully understand. I spent a ton of time by myself. Why was it bothering me today?

And it wasn't like I was actually by myself. Andras and Raziel were still very, very here. In fact, they'd been bickering on the coffee table for the last twenty minutes. I'd mostly tuned it out because... I mean, when *weren't* they bickering? They reminded me of a lab partner I'd had in sophomore chemistry. Everyone had called us an old married couple because we were *constantly* sniping and arguing. We drove each other up a wall, right up until the day of our final exam. I still couldn't put my finger on exactly when the switch had flipped, only that we'd been up to our usual bitching on the way into the lecture hall... and after the exam, we'd gone straight to his dorm and fucked each other senseless.

We'd dated for two years after that, to the surprise of absolutely no one except for us.

I chuckled at the memory as I listened to the angel and demon getting into it.

"Oh, *this* again?" Raziel groaned theatrically. "For the last time, we are *not* taking anyone to speed dating. Not again."

"Why the fuck not?" Andras gave an irritated snap of his wings. "D'you know how many people you can weed out when you're meeting them like—" He snapped his fingers rapidly.

Raziel planted his hands on his hips and glared at his partner. "You can't learn anything but superficial nonsense in five minutes!"

"You're superficial nonsense," Andras muttered.

Raziel just huffed and shook his head.

I bit back a laugh. Yeah, assuming they didn't kill each other, and assuming angels and demons even had sex, it was probably only a matter of time before this pair wound up fucking just like Dominic and I had.

I just hoped it didn't happen while they were still on my shoulders. Or in my bed. Eww.

On my phone, I flipped to my text app, ready to send Cory a message about *LOL, I swear these two are one argument away from screwing*.

But I froze. Thumbs hovering over the keyboard, I hesitated. Maybe it wasn't a good idea. I'd monopolized his

Saturday, and he'd said he had things to do today. Plus we'd be together again tomorrow. He didn't need me to—

Cory started typing.

My heart jumped into my throat. A million possibilities rained down in my mind. Was he canceling for tomorrow? Did he want Andras and Raziel to help him figure out his profile? Though... he'd honestly done more for mine than they had, so he probably didn't need any help there. Was he... What *was* on his mind?

The typing icon disappeared.

A moment later, it reappeared.

I swallowed. My heart pounded as I waited for him to send something. Seriously, what was he trying to say?

But after a minute or so, the icon vanished again.

And this time, it didn't come back.

Cory

This is pointless. I'm a coward.

I exited the text app for probably the fortieth time and laid my phone on my chest. Then I stared up at my bedroom ceiling.

The ghosts of long-quieted creaks and muffled moans needled at me, and I closed my eyes and rubbed my hands over my face.

The way our apartments were laid out, Matt's bedroom was conveniently over the top of mine. Noise-canceling headphones had saved my sanity on more than one occasion, but not entirely. Even if I could shut out the sounds of the man of my dreams getting laid right above my head, I couldn't shut out the mental images. It was almost a relief that he'd been in a dry spell for a while; I felt bad for him, and I hated that he was miserable and frustrated, but my sanity needed a break from that period when he'd been getting fucked *very* regularly.

Admittedly, I brought some of that on myself. There'd been nights when I'd skipped the headphones and let myself listen. I couldn't fucking resist sometimes. Matt was vocal in bed, and the way his floor and furniture told it, he liked things on the rough side. One night, a strained, border-ing-on-a-sob, *"God, yeah, harder,"* had filtered down to my room, and I'd come before either of them had.

Matt would be *mortified* if he knew.

And what would he feel if he knew what I'd been trying work up the courage to text him? If he knew I'd been vacillating between wishing I could bow out of tomorrow and...

Ugh. Christ. Either way, that would be awkward as all hell. I knew where we stood, so what was the point? Why make things weird with my friend? Because at the end of the day, even if I couldn't have him as the lover I so desperately wanted, I still had him as my friend.

Admitting I loved him would just complicate things.

Matt

I'd say one thing for Cory's version of my profile—it was getting more positive attention than the old one. By the time

I decided to head to bed, I had some new matches on the various apps, and a handful of messages.

I'd also read and reread what he'd written, and every time, that weird restlessness kicked in even harder. The words were just so... *me*. How did Cory have a better handle on who I was and what I wanted than I did?

And why did I keep hoping that the next person to swipe right would be him?

That was stupid. Completely and utterly ridiculous.

But... it was also driving me out my head. Cory and I spent time at both of our apartments doing all the things he'd described in my profile. When our schedules lined up, we'd go to the gym together. He'd taken me kayaking last summer after his sister had canceled at the last minute, and we'd talked about doing it again this year. We even grocery shopped together sometimes, ostensibly because there was limited parking at our preferred supermarket, but really because I just liked having someone come along with me.

I liked having *him* come along with me.

And that part he'd included about cooking together— fuck. That had hit me in the feels. Some of my best memories were of the two of us laughing as we navigated effortlessly around each other in his kitchen or mine. Nothing in the world compared to the flutter I'd get in my chest when I'd have him taste something I was cooking, and he'd get one of those expressions or make one of those sounds that was *almost* sexual.

The thought of cooking with someone else the way I did with him...

Or of *him* doing it with someone else...

Jesus. I couldn't even describe the way that hurt.

Cory

Lying in bed that night, I tracked Matt's movements on the floor above me. His routine had been weirdly comforting on some of my loneliest nights. Even though I couldn't see him and he had no idea I could hear him, there'd been something soothing about listening to him move around in his room before settling into bed. As if it were a reminder that someone I cared about was close by. Not in the same room or even on the same floor, but at least in the same building. On those really lonely nights, I took what I could get.

Sometimes I wondered if he stayed up reading. A paperback? Or did he take his work to bed? Maybe some doomscrolling?

Tonight...

Tonight, all I could think about was how bad I wanted to be there with him. I was lonelier than I'd been in I didn't know how long, and hearing his floor creak under his weight, hearing him settle into his bed, hearing the stillness that always followed—it just made my chest hurt. I wanted to be there with him.

It wasn't even sex I wanted right now. Yeah, I'd absolutely fuck Matt without a second thought, but what I needed in this moment wasn't physical. I just wanted to be close to him.

Above me, the floor creaked with his usual path across the room. Then the bed announced he'd climbed in.

Part of me wished he had someone with him now. Part of me was grateful he didn't. Did that make me a bad friend? Probably. But there it was.

I couldn't stop my mind from whirling with thoughts of

Matt as he settled in above me. What if he had been with someone? Did he sleep curled against his partner? Did he like being the big spoon or the little spoon? Did he drift away from them in the middle of the night, only to cuddle up close to them in the morning?

And how much more would it suck when there was another set of footsteps moving around up there? When it wasn't just the sounds of a one-night stand, but that of someone whose name was on the lease? When they sometimes didn't have sex and just went to bed?

I squeezed my eyes shut.

Today had been harder than it should've been. Tomorrow promised to be more of the same.

Would I be an asshole if I bailed? Maybe. Maybe not. I had to take care of myself, too.

But I knew me. I knew I'd go.

Because at the end of the day, I wanted Matt to find happiness.

Even if it was killing me to help him find it with someone else.

CHAPTER 8

MATT

It was almost eleven, and I hadn't heard from Cory.

Should I text him? Why am I afraid to text him?

All I knew was every time I looked at my text app, I expected to see that typing icon. I still had no idea what he'd meant to say last night. Maybe he'd just opened the wrong window? Like he was actually intending to write something to someone else? Or he'd left the window open with a text half-written?

Except... no. He'd started and stopped multiple times. I didn't imagine in that time he'd failed to notice which window he was typing in.

I still didn't know what that was all about, and for reasons I couldn't quite explain, I couldn't bring myself to make contact. Not now. For the five years we'd been friends and neighbors, neither of us had hesitated to knock on the other's door, but I was suddenly a coward who couldn't send a text. What the hell?

Probably because I was irrationally certain that if I texted, the response would be *Sorry, can't make it. Have fun without me!*

I bit back a groan. I hoped he wasn't bailing today. I hated leaning on him, and my God, I owed him big time, but there was no way I could handle this shopping trip with just... *them.*

Though at the moment, only one of them was around.

I scanned my living room. "Where's Raziel?"

"Taking his fifteen." From where he'd sat on the back of the couch, another unfurled scroll in his hand, Andras huffed. "I need a break from him, too, so..." He made a shooing motion.

Great. So they weren't taking their breaks together? I could get rid of one but not the other? Awesome. Just what I needed.

I sat in the armrest and sipped my coffee, watching the tiny demon furrowing his brow and peering at the paper. Gesturing at it with my coffee cup, I said, "Is that a different assignment? Or our agreement again?"

"It's our briefing for this assignment." Andras didn't take his eyes off what he was reading. "All the rules and whatnot."

I cocked a brow. "Haven't you already read it like fifty times?"

"Seventy-one." At that he looked up at me and offered a sharky grin. "But you know what they say—the devil's in the details."

I groaned and covered my face with my free hand. "For fuck's sake. *Really?*"

His chuckle was downright, well, demonic.

I just lowered my hand and brought up my coffee for a sip.

Andras snickered again. Then he sighed and started rolling up the scroll. "One of us has to know all the details.

Isn't like Raziel ever reads it." He huffed and shook his head.

It was my turn for a chuckle. "You two sound like an old married couple. You know that?"

His head snapped toward me. "What? Fuck off."

"You do!" I laughed. "Nobody bickers that much unless they've been married a while."

He muttered something I didn't catch, but then he sighed, and the sound was almost wistful. "We might as well be married for all we work together."

I cocked a brow. "Yeah? You like working with him?"

Andras gave one of those shrugs that was clearly meant to look more flippant than he actually felt. "He's an utter bampot half the time, but..." The faintest hint of fondness crept into his voice and expression. "We make a good pair. Most of the time."

"Most of the time?" I said with a laugh.

"You've heard him," Andras explained. "He's a wanker."

I just chuckled, but it faded. "I've had that with someone before. I miss it."

"Miss it?" Andras scoffed. "Give me that electric flyswatter, and when he comes back, I'll show you how much I miss him."

I laughed. "Whatever you say, man."

Minutes later, Raziel returned, looking refreshed and way too chipper. Better than hangry, I supposed.

"Well." He smiled brightly. "Should we be off soon? The shops should be open by now, yes?"

"Yeah, yeah, we're..." I glanced at my watch. "Just waiting for Cory."

Cory, who was probably about to cancel. If I opened my

text app, those three dots would almost definitely be there, indicating he was typing… something. Knowing him, a tactful way of bowing out instead of wasting more of his time helping my pathetic ass get laid. And could I blame him? After he'd spent all day yesterday with me, he was well within his rights to—

My phone pinged with a text notification, and I yanked it out of my pocket so fast I almost fumbled with it.

Ready to go when you are.

The relief that crashed over me was mind-blowing. This was just a shopping trip, for God's sake, but… I was really, really glad Cory was still on board.

And it wasn't just because I didn't know how to hold on to my sanity through this without him.

Truth was, I just…

Wanted him there.

"I think it looks lovely!" Raziel declared, fluttering so enthusiastically beside me that he was kicking up a breeze. "It's perfect!"

"Nah." Andras lounged on my shoulder, because of course he did. "It ain't slutty enough."

I eyed him in the dressing room's full-length mirror. "Slutty enough? Really?"

"You want to get laid, don't ya?"

Okay, he had me there. "I do, yes," I said cautiously, "but define 'slutty enough'? Because I'm not going out in a mesh shirt."

Andras shrugged. "Who says you have to wear a shirt at all?"

I rolled my eyes. "Shirts are not negotiable."

He scoffed and crossed his arms, giving his wings an

emphatic and irritated snap. "Let's see how you feel about that in"—he pantomimed checking a watch—"twenty-nine days."

"Twenty-nine—" But then the piece clicked. Twenty-nine days until the revised agreement shifted to the original and I couldn't escape my annoying companions at all. With a sigh of defeat, I let my shoulders drop, which caused Andras to take a satisfying tumble before he caught himself on my sleeve. "Fine. Let's... Let's talk, uh..." My cheeks heated. "I'll *consider* sluttier. But this is okay, isn't it?" I motioned at the mirror.

This was my fifth trip into this changing room since we'd arrived at the ghost town of a shopping mall downtown. Trying to please these two was... an ordeal. Especially since, once we were in the privacy of a dressing room and they were allowed to show themselves, they had *opinions*.

A simple navy blue jacket over my plain white T-shirt and jeans? Too sloppy according to Raziel. Too boring according to Andras.

The skintight faux leather pants Andras had insisted I put on were obscenely revealing according to Raziel.

The all-white suit—complete with purple tie and pocket square—chosen by Raziel had prompted a sneer from Andras, but he hadn't even needed to pipe up on that one. I'd vetoed it before I pulled it off the rack, and I'd only tried it on so Raziel would shut up about it. No. Just *no*.

And now, as I stood here in a pair of black pants with a muted green Henley, my winged consultants were once again at an impasse.

Fortunately, there was a third voter whose opinion I valued significantly more than theirs.

I reached for the door and waited for that barely perceptible crackle of energy that zinged over my nerve endings whenever Andras and Raziel vanished. Just to be safe, I glanced to either side to make sure they'd vacated. They had. That, or they were being so still and silent I couldn't see or hear them, but yeah, right—that would be the day.

Safely devoid of shoulder passengers, I pushed open the door and stepped out into the hallway.

And for a few seconds, I lost my train of thought.

Cory was, as he'd been at the last three stores, kicked back in one of the chairs, his relaxed posture not unlike the way Andras often chilled on my shoulder. He had one long leg crossed over the other, his rainbow Chuck Taylors bright against the backdrop of his black jeans. He hadn't bothered with his contacts today, unaware of how incredibly sexy he was in those black-rimmed glasses.

Fortunately, he was also unaware of the way my breath stuttered and my balance wavered. Straightening in the chair, he gave me an appraising down-up. "Ooh, I like this."

I shook myself and looked down at the Henley and pants. "You think it works?"

"Definitely." He rose, sliding his phone into his back pocket as he looked me up and down again. When he reached the shirt, he pursed his lips. "I'm not completely sold on the color, though."

"No?"

"It's... I mean, it's not *bad*. But I think..." He scowled. "I don't know. And I'm not sure what color would be better?"

I studied him. "So... should I... grab a few different colors and try them?"

Cory's smile made me forget all about colors and clothes. "Why don't I go grab a few off the rack while you try the next thing? What size is that again?"

"I, uh..." He expected me to remember that? I gestured over my shoulder. "Check the tag?"

He motioned for me to turn around, and when his fingers grazed the back of my neck, I hoped he didn't notice the goose bumps springing up in their wake. Thank God he couldn't hear my thoughts, because we didn't need to talk about why some voice in my head wanted me to tell him to tug harder on my collar.

All too soon, he let go of the shirt. "Got it. Okay, I'll be back in a second."

"Okay. Sure. I'll, uh..." What was I doing?

Right then, a saleswoman came by with some hangers in her hand. "Oh hey! How are things going over—" She glanced into the dressing room, did a double take, then looked around. "Oh, did your friend leave?"

"My..." I gestured at Cory. "I'm here with him."

She blinked. "But... I heard you talking to someone in..." She pointed at the dressing room.

Oh. Fuck. Uh...

"He was just FaceTiming one of our friends." Cory huffed a laugh and rolled his eyes. "Apparently *my* input isn't sufficient."

Good save, my friend. Good save.

"Oh." The saleswoman smiled. "That makes sense. Can I take anything out of there for you?"

"No, that's fine. I still need to try most of it."

"Okay! Just let me know if you need any help!"

If she only knew that I probably had more help than I could ever need. Certainly more help than I could ever want.

And the second I'd closed the dressing room door again, they were back.

"So, we're in agreement?" Raziel said. "A keeper?"

Andras groaned, lounging on my shoulder like an after-image of Cory. "We're not in agreement. Sluttier!"

I rolled my eyes. "Would you two..." I gestured at the clothing rack, which was where they perched whenever I was changing. Technically, I could pull a shirt on or off without dislodging either of them. I still wasn't sure how that worked. Celestial beings had some strange physical properties, after all. I could peel off a shirt without so much as ruffling a feather, but I could dislodge them with a well-placed smack or a drop of my shoulder.

Whatever the case, I'd asked them to park their asses over there while I was changing clothes. I could grudgingly accept them being in here with me, but I didn't need them literally sitting on my bare shoulders while I was getting dressed. That was just too weird.

Right. As if the USS *Too Fucking Weird* hadn't sailed a *long* time ago.

With a sigh, I took off the green Henley.

"There, see?" Andras motioned at me. "Slutty!"

I froze, then looked down at myself. Rolling my eyes again, I muttered, "I'm not going out shirtless to pick up guys."

"Fine." He crossed his arms. "Don't whinge at me when you've got blue balls again."

I threw the Henley at him, earning me a satisfying squawk as he tumbled off the rack and onto the hangers below.

"Ah, piss off, you fucking tadger!" There was some rattling of hangers. Then he flew up to the rack again, sat down and glared at me.

A few inches away, Raziel smothered a laugh. Andras rolled his eyes and flipped him off. When I snickered, he aimed the gesture at me.

Still chuckling, I picked up the Henley, put it on the hanger, and then looked through the other options I'd brought in here. It was a lot, too—I was seriously starting to regret letting Andras and Raziel know about the notepad function on my smartphone. They'd made me a list, and probably a third of that list—the most I could bring into the dressing room at one time—had come in here with me. Several things had already gone back out, having been vetoed by Cory, me, or both.

I had yet to find anything both Andras and Raziel agreed on, whether as a yea or a nay, and I was starting to think I never would. Because Jesus Christ, these two had seriously opposing tastes. Raziel liked dignified and even formal, with perfect lines and muted colors (aside from the purple he'd paired with that white suit monstrosity). Andras preferred things louder—brighter colors, higher contrast, and of course, more skin showing. I was almost afraid to find out what disaster of an outfit would get both of their approvals.

A quiet knock startled me.

"I've got some shirts," Cory called through the door. "These colors might work."

Without thinking about it, I opened the door. There was that subtle crackle on the air, like a zip of static electricity, letting me know Andras and Raziel had vacated.

Or maybe that was my brain skidding to a halt because of the little hitch in Cory's breath. Unless I'd imagined that? Along with that down-up that didn't seem to be anything like when he was appraising a new outfit choice. Especially when it lingered for half a heartbeat in the vicinity of my belt.

Before I could figure out if I'd imagined it, Cory cleared his throat, blushing brightly, and shoved half a dozen shirts into my hands. He sounded hoarse as he said, "These, uh... These should work better than..." He gestured past me.

"Right. Yeah." I swallowed, trying not to drop the clothes. "Thanks. I'll, uh..." I nodded into the dressing room. "Give me a minute?"

"Sure. Of course." His smile had an edge of panic that I couldn't make sense of, but I didn't stick around to try to figure it out.

Like the freaked-out coward I was, I stepped back into the dressing room and pulled the door safely shut behind me. Why was my heart beating this fast? And why was I out of breath?

And had Cory seriously—

"Well, get on with it, then," Andras barked impatiently from my left shoulder. "You going to stand there and hug those things or try them on?"

I pushed out a breath through my nose and stared up at the ceiling.

"We've only got a few hours," Raziel said from my right shoulder, his tone cheerful but prodding. "Come on, now. Let's see what he picked out!"

Closing my eyes, I sighed. I was suddenly exhausted. I didn't want to try on anything else. I didn't want to fuck around with hookup app profiles or whatever other fresh hell the dating scene could offer. I wanted Cory to look at me like that again.

I wanted Cory to want me.

I wanted to believe that, in that moment when I'd caught him off-guard, he'd let a mask slip. Let it show that he *did* want me.

Yeah, right. I pushed myself off the door. *Cory can do a hell of a lot better than me.*

So, no, I wasn't motivated at all to put myself out there now. I never was when I'd been around Cory.

But the breezes kicked up by fluttering wings beside my

head reminded me that not only did I need to put myself out there, I needed to do so successfully in the next twenty-nine days. Otherwise my reputation, my career, and my shot at love or even a random hookup would go up in smoke.

I am never drinking with a fae again. Goddammit.

Ah well. It was what it was.

Time to put on something that might attract someone with lower standards than Cory's.

CHAPTER 9

CORY

When we'd first arrived at this particular store, I'd so wanted to offer to come into the dressing room with Matt. I mean, a boy could dream, right? About things like changing clothes turning into taking off clothes and then... Well. I didn't want to be banned from this store for life, but a dressing room hookup with Matt would be totally worth it.

Now that we'd been here for over an hour, I was grateful for the door between us, not to mention the arguing and bickering on the other side. I needed a minute, damn it.

Leaning back in the chair, I closed my eyes and took some slow, deep breaths as I tried to will my pulse back down to something safe. Didn't matter that he was in a dressing room—I had *not* been ready for that man to step out without a shirt on.

Get a grip, I ordered myself. *It isn't like you've never seen him shirtless before.*

That was true. I'd almost fallen off a treadmill or dropped a dumbbell on my foot on more than one occasion when he'd taken off his shirt at the gym. When he'd been helping our landlord fix the tiles on the stairs last summer, I was lucky I hadn't gone ass over teakettle down said stairs. And when we went kayaking... *Lord*.

So I was used to losing my mind when Matt lost his shirt. I just hadn't been expecting it *today*. As it was, I'd already been climbing the walls with frustration over why we were here and what we were doing. I could gaslight myself into believing the end goal today was to break the spell so Andras and Raziel left, but that never lasted long. Not when the end meant means that were seriously tough for me to stomach.

Then for him to fling open that door and stand there in front of me, half-dressed in snug, low-slung black pants that sat just right on his hips? Those flat abs and salt-and-pepper treasure trail on full display? *Sir*. How dare you?

I rubbed the bridge of my nose and exhaled. This was ridiculous. Matt was my friend, and yes, I was attracted to him, and yes, I would absolutely see this through to the end because I cared about him.

But oh my God, the *instant* I had a few hours to myself? *Gentlemen of Grindr, my body is ready.*

In the dressing room, the bickering had started up again, so Matt must've been dressed. As I listened, I pulled myself together, since he'd probably be stepping out to get my opinion before too much longer.

"How is that sluttier?" Andras demanded. "It's... for fuck's sake, man. It's *purple*."

"What the hell is wrong with purple?" Matt's voice was full of exasperation. "Don't tell me you're also the Angel of Toxic Masculinity."

I smothered a laugh, especially at the sputtering rage coming from Andras. "I am not an angel of anything!"

"That's not exactly a denial about the toxic masculinity part."

Whatever Andras muttered in response, I didn't catch. Raziel said something, too, and it was Matt's turn for a muffled mutter. I pressed my lips together, trying desperately not to laugh. As much as this was all stressing Matt out, it *was* hilarious at times.

There was some movement, and then the squeak of a hanger moving on the rack. More movement, followed by a sharp "No" from Matt. "I'm getting *his* opinion first."

A second later, the door swung open again, and Matt stepped out. He wasn't wearing the purple Henley anymore. Instead, he had on the khaki one, with two of the three dark brown buttons open below his throat. I'd grabbed that shirt as an afterthought, thinking he'd prefer the blue, the dark gray, or even the purple.

He had absolutely no business being that sexy—that spectacularly fuckable—in that shirt.

I gulped. "Oh. I... wasn't sure you'd like..." I looked him up and down, pretending to appraise his outfit instead of just drinking him in because I wanted to. "That looks... amazing on you."

Matt's eyebrows shot up. "It does?"

"Yeah." Where was my breath? "That color..." I cleared my throat and smiled. "That's, uh... That's definitely a keeper."

"Oh." He looked down at himself as some pink bloomed in his cheeks. "I wasn't sure about it, but once I put it on..." He trailed off as he picked a phantom piece of lint off the shirt. Then he smiled at me. "Great. Finally found a winner."

"Definitely a winner."

We exchanged smiles, and as he disappeared back into the dressing room, it dawned on me that the shirt would probably look even better on someone's bedroom floor.

On *my* bedroom floor.

But that isn't going to happen, so just stop torturing yourself with—

"I approve," Raziel declared.

"Aye," Andras agreed. "It ain't slutty, but it'll do."

"Are you serious?" Matt sounded completely stunned. There was silence, but I assumed they were nodding or otherwise expressing their agreement. Then Matt huffed a quiet laugh. "And here I thought I'd never find anything you'd both like that I was willing to wear out in public."

An intrusive thought almost came tumbling out of my mouth: *Don't wear it in public—wear it at my place.*

I sank back into the chair and wiped a hand over my face. Staring up at the ceiling, I wondered exactly what I'd done in a past life to deserve this. Assassinated a king, maybe? Lit the fire that burned the Library of Alexandria? Or maybe some way-back ancestor had earned the family a generational curse by screwing over a fae?

In the dressing room, Raziel chirped, "You know, perhaps we should find you some better underwear, too?"

"Better... underwear?" Matt's disbelief was almost palpable. "My underwear is fine. What do—do I even want to know what that means?"

Andras barked a laugh. "Something *slutty!*"

I closed my eyes and groaned.

Thanks a lot, great-great-great-great-grandancestor.

Matt ended up leaving that store with two bags containing several shirts and a couple of pairs of pants. We were still going to check out a few more places, including getting him some shoes, but fortunately, our next stop was the food court. I was starving, and I also needed a break from, well, everything.

From the way Matt's jaw was working on the way out, I was pretty sure I wasn't the only one. I couldn't tell if he was getting hangry or if he'd just had it up to here with Andras and Raziel, but lunch would resolve both of those problems.

The food court was about as depressing as the rest of the mall. About a third of the restaurants were shuttered, and those that remained were staffed by employees who looked like they were a hundred percent done with humanity. I understood that; I'd done my time in food service, and I was grateful that was over.

Matt and I both ended up ordering smoothies and sandwiches from the same place. He insisted on paying, and the twenty he dropped in the tip jar got both of the weary kids behind the counter to smile. That was to say nothing about what it did to my pulse and my balance.

Oh my God, would you stop being so amazing, you asshole?

We found a table that was reasonably clean, sat down, and started eating.

Halfway through his sandwich, a calmer and less aggravated Matt met my gaze across our small table. "Thank you again. For doing this. I'm..." He chuckled, shaking his head. "I'm so lost when it comes to all of this."

"Nah, you're probably just overthinking it."

He cocked a brow.

I shrugged. "You should see me trying to figure out what to wear to go out or even to meet someone." I laughed. "Even when I know for a fact whatever I put on is coming off two minutes after I walk through the door."

Matt's eyes widened, and I'll be damned if he didn't

blush. He had to clear his throat before he asked, "Is, uh... Is that right?"

"What can I say?" I plucked a pickle slice off my sandwich. "It's easy when it's someone else. When it's me..." I grimaced and then popped the pickle into my mouth.

Matt watched me, and then he sat back in his chair and exhaled. "At least it's not just me."

"Yeah?"

He nodded. "I can look at a guy and immediately decide if he looks put together, if he's got a sense of style, if he's hot—like, I have taste, you know? But when it comes to dressing myself?" He laughed dryly as he reached for his smoothie. "I'm just lucky my line of work requires suits. Those are easy. Everything else..." He trailed off, shaking his head.

Lord, the last thing we needed right now was suited Matt parading through my head. I'd seen him dressed for work, not to mention plenty of mutual friends' weddings, so I had an *extensive* catalog of sartorially pornographic Matt-themed images to choose from.

I took a quick gulp from my own drink to cool down and wet my suddenly dry mouth. "For what it's worth, I've never looked askance at the way you dress." I gave a haughty laugh. "Not something I can say about *most* of our social circle."

Matt snorted. "Meow."

I shrugged unapologetically.

He just laughed, which was a relief. Didn't do much to keep my pulse in a safe range, but it was still good to see some humor breaking through. I hated how stressed he was right now.

I shifted in my chair. "Well, um, now that we've

zhuzhed up your wardrobe..." I grinned. "Time to put it into action, right?"

He peered at me suspiciously. "Put it into action... how?"

"Any chance you want to try a club?"

Matt stared incredulously at me. "A club? Like... a dance club?"

"No, honey. A country club." I rolled my eyes. "Yes, of course a dance club."

He blinked a few times. "Have you forgotten who you're talking to?" He gestured at himself. "Look at me!"

Oh, he didn't have to tell me twice. I never missed an opportunity to look at him.

"Matt." I tsked. "You're the kind of guy who turns heads in clubs."

He arched an eyebrow. "Why? Because half the people there think someone's dad just walked in?"

"More like someone's daddy."

Matt tilted his head, eyeing me as if I'd lost my mind or spoken in Martian.

I laughed, nudging him under the table with my foot. "Dude. You're hot. And the club I go to, there's plenty of guys there who are in their thirties and up. It isn't a college bar."

He pursed his lips. "That, um... That really doesn't sound like my scene."

I raised an eyebrow. "And running out the clock before Andras and Raziel are visible 24/7 is?"

He winced. Then he slumped in his chair and sighed. "Oh God. I'm going to a club, aren't I?"

"Yes, you are." I nudged him again. "Come on! It'll be fun!" *Even if it'll be absolute torture for me, especially if you and some rando start making out on the dancefloor and—* I cleared my throat. "Tell you what—try the hookup apps this week. Put yourself out there. See if you have any luck. And if you don't reel anyone in by Saturday night?" I grinned and sing-songed, "Then we go dancing!"

Matt looked at me like I'd suggested we go get drug-free root canals for funsies. But little by little, he seemed to surrender to the idea. He didn't warm up to it, but he didn't fight it.

"Okay. If I don't have any luck, then..." He let his currently unoccupied shoulders sag. "Then I guess we're going dancing."

I grinned triumphantly, but beneath the surface...

Oh, holy hell.

What did I just sign up for?

"I'm telling you," Andras declared. "Make. It. Sluttier."

Naturally, that had Raziel ranting and raving yet again about how respectable and dignified was the way to go. They shouted back and forth, waving arms and wings, while Matt pinched the bridge of his nose and probably imagined tasing both of them.

I lowered my phone, which I'd been using to get some photos for his various profiles. We'd been at this for all of twenty minutes in Matt's living room, and he looked absolutely miserable, which definitely didn't do his photos any favors.

Then... inspiration hit me.

I cleared my throat. "Hey, I've got an idea."

The angel and demon turned curious looks on me. Matt watched me, his face screaming of desperation to get out of this situation.

I motioned toward the windows. "The lighting outside is perfect. Maybe if we go over to that park behind the movie theater, we can get some better shots?"

Matt lifted an eyebrow. "It's, um... It's usually a little crowded this time of day, isn't it?"

"On a Sunday afternoon? Absolutely." I shrugged. "But I'm sure we can find a spot up against the trees or something."

He studied me. Then understanding seemed to dawn, and for the first time since we'd returned to his apartment, something like relief filled his expression. "I'll get my keys."

Five minutes later, we were in the park along with dozens of people, dogs, and bicycles. There was noise and activity coming from everywhere, and we both nearly got run over by children and bikes as we crossed over to the hedges surrounding the park's garden.

And despite all the activity and moving hazards, Matt already seemed a million times more relaxed than he'd been in the apartment.

"It's a little chaotic out here," I told him, "but I figured being out in the open with people, you wouldn't have to deal with... you know..."

He pushed out a breath and rolled his unoccupied shoulders. "It was a great idea. Another minute or two, and I was going to..." He pursed his lips. "Hell, I don't know what I was going to do. But the flyswatter was sounding more and more tempting."

I snorted. "I can still Amazon Prime the electric one."

"Might not be a bad idea." He glanced at me with a lopsided grin. "I'll pay you back if you order me one."

"Hey, don't threaten me with a good time. I won't even make you pay me back as long as I get to zap one of them."

The way he laughed almost made me stumble. He'd been understandably wound tight all day, and seeing him break through that and laugh like he did when we were hanging out and relaxing? Oh my God. Shame I didn't have my phone up in that moment. That photo would've had so many people swiping right that it would probably crash all the apps.

I muffled a cough and gestured at the hedge. "Think this will work for a backdrop?"

Matt paused to give it a look, and he scanned the rest of our surroundings too.

While I was hardly God's gift to photography, I recognized beauty when I saw it. And in that moment, as a ray of warm, late afternoon light landed on the side of his face while his gaze was fixed on something, Matt was absolutely gorgeous. I might've missed that moment of unrestrained laughter breaking through like the sun piercing a storm cloud, I was fast enough to get my phone up and focused this time.

The snap of the camera turned his head, and he peered at me. "What?"

"Nothing." I shrugged, pretending my heart wasn't suddenly and inexplicably going way too fast. "Just, uh..." I gestured with my phone. "Not every photo you use needs to be posed, does it?"

He furrowed his brow as his eyes flicked toward the phone. "Do I get to see it?"

I wasn't sure why I hesitated. Because I was afraid the photo would give something away? I was an idiot. Face inexplicably burning, I pulled up the photo and showed it to him.

He leaned in, oblivious to his body heat brushing against me, and he looked at the screen. "Oh. Man. That *is* a good picture." Now he was the one blushing. "I, um... Maybe I'll use that one."

I smiled, hoping he took it as friendly and maybe a touch shy, and not even a little bit because I had some seriously mixed feelings about the possibility of this photo attracting the man of his dreams. I was happy to help him, but—

God, stop it, Cory. He's not interested. Just help him find a man and then go find one for yourself.

That sounded like a great idea.

First things first...

I gestured at the hedge. "So, right here?"

"Sure. Yeah." He stepped toward it. "Just, um right up against it? Or...?" He inclined his head and raised his eyebrows, clearly waiting for me to give him some instruction.

"There is good. Or... Hmm. Maybe a little to the..." I gestured to his left. He took a half step to the side, shifting out of the direct sunlight and letting a softer shadow slide over his face. "Perfect." I brought up my phone. I debated stepping closer for a better composition, but I wasn't so sure I could handle that right then. Instead, I stayed put and zoomed in a little.

Cowardice, thy name is Cory.

Matt watched me. Or, well, the camera. His expression was stoic—the kind of look I'd have expected in a portrait for his law firm's website—but with an undercurrent of nerves. As if he wasn't quite sure what to do with his face.

"Maybe this would've been easier if we'd stayed in your apartment." I looked at him over the phone and smirked. "With Andras yelling at you to look sluttier."

That got exactly the effect I'd hoped for—a bright, unrestrained laugh.

Snap. Snap. Snap.

Christ, you're beautiful.

Matt rolled his eyes, and even as he started to pull himself together, he was still smiling.

Snap. Snap. Snap.

The smile fell a little, and he cocked his head. "What?"

"Hmm?"

"You're taking pictures already? We're not even... like..." He gestured as if he couldn't find the word.

"Hey, you want them to look natural, right? Nothing looks more natural than candid."

He held my gaze, studying me as if he'd just learned something about me and wanted to tug at the new thread. "I didn't know you were into photography."

"I mean, I'm not, like—" *Snap. Snap.* "I'm okay at it, I guess? But I've never done much with it. I can just tell a stiff-looking, unnaturally posed photo, you know?"

He seemed to consider that. "Okay, I can see that. But I've seen what you post on social media. You've got a better eye than I ever will."

Warmth rushed through me that I tried my damnedest to ignore even as I took a couple more photos of him looking relaxed but interested. "Thanks," I said. "I've, um... I've done it as a hobby off and on over the years. Haven't had anything printed in a long time, though." *Snap.* "Maybe I should do that."

The smile that brought out of him—oh, my God. *Snap, snap, fucking snap.*

"You should," he said softly. "I'd love to see them if you do."

I could only imagine the look on my own face right then. If the heat in my face and the flutter in my chest were anything to go by, I probably wasn't being subtle about anything.

Shame he wouldn't see it or do anything about it if I wrote *Matt, I want you* across my forehead, but I shook that thought away, and we continued with our impromptu photo shoot.

As we went on, I tried to stay upbeat and enjoy this moment with my friend. Deep down, though, it was hard to ignore the miserable feeling in the pit of my stomach.

Because I couldn't forget what we were doing. Why we were here. What Matt hoped to accomplish with my help.

I really, really hoped the photos, the new clothes, and the rejuvenated profiles helped Matt find someone. I hoped he texted me to say, *"Don't worry about Saturday night!"* and I wouldn't have to follow through with taking him to a club.

Because while I was committed to doing and being whatever he needed...

I wasn't so sure I could handle that after all.

CHAPTER 10

MATT

Spoiler: I did not have any luck on the apps that week.

As Saturday night rapidly approached—we were down to hours now—I kept trying, just on that off chance I stumbled across the right guy to save me from a night of clubbing. My lack of success *wasn't* for lack of effort.

It also wasn't for lack of... well, "help" might've been a generous way to describe it.

"Does he bring his own paper bag?" Andras pointed his tail at a Grindr profile. "Or d'you have to give him one?"

"A paper bag?" Raziel scoffed. "My dear, now who isn't reading the briefings? It's called a condom, and it's not made of paper, it's made of—"

"Not for his willy," Andras retorted. "For his feckin' face."

That got a startled gasp out of Raziel. "Well... That's just not very nice, is it?"

At that, Andras had flown off my shoulder so he was in Raziel's view, and gestured wildly at himself as if to say *"Have you forgotten who you're talking to?"* Then the demon returned to my shoulder and flopped down unceremoniously.

"Ow!" I shrugged a little dislodge him. "You have got the boniest ass, I swear."

Andras whapped me with his tail, so I brushed him completely off my shoulder, earning me a satisfied yelp and some swearing. He landed on the other couch cushion, so he wasn't any worse for the wear, but he sure was mad.

"What the fuck?" He flew back up, snapped his wings next to my ear, and sat down dramatically again as he muttered, "Wanker."

"I'll do it again," I warned.

He huffed. "Just swipe left and keep looking."

I rolled my eyes. I did end up swiping left on that guy, but not because of his looks. Physically, there was nothing unattractive about him. I was trying not to be too shallow anyway—even with guys I might only hook up with—but really, I had no idea what Andras's issue with him was. I just wasn't into the guy because he sounded like a pretentious dick.

The next profile was more to Andras's liking, but of course, Raziel disagreed.

"Look at the background of his photos!" The angel clicked his tongue. "Look at... Do you want someone who takes selfies in front of piles of laundry? And... my God, young man. Wash the dishes once in a—"

"He ain't looking for someone to do his washing," Andras said. "Long as he's got clean sheets, who cares?"

I rubbed my forehead. Would *"I have a headache"* be a valid excuse to bail on tonight? Because it wouldn't be a lie.

"Quit perving on his housekeeping," Andras groused, "and look at those abs! That arse! And a mouth like that is probably great for—"

"Andras." Raziel was just outside my peripheral vision, but I swore heat rose beside that shoulder. Was he blushing that hot? "There is more to a man than just—" He sputtered a bit. "Yes, he's pretty, but the background is unattractive."

He did have a point. While I tried not to judge guys based on the backgrounds of impromptu selfies, those backgrounds could tell a story. Or raise red flags. Like the one a few profiles ago who'd carelessly—or deliberately, I couldn't decide—taken a photo in front of several items that screamed white supremacist. I had, of course, swiped left on him, but not before sending his profile to a sorcerer friend I'd known since law school. They wouldn't hurt the guy or anything. They wouldn't do anything illegal. They were, however, an expert troll who would happily catfish the guy until the end of time, wasting his time and keeping him occupied. He wouldn't be anyone's problem as long as their endless repertoire of profiles kept leading him on.

Ethical? Eh, I didn't lose any sleep over it. Fuck Nazis. Or, well, don't fuck them. Catfish them instead.

I continued perusing profiles until a shirtless pic didn't just catch my eye, it made my brain skid to a halt. The broad shoulders, the narrow waist, that ass—oh. Hell.

I wasn't the only one who thought so.

"Ooh, look at the arse on that one," Andras said.

"My, my, he's certainly pretty." Raziel sighed. "Pity we can't see his face."

I swallowed, which took some work, since my mouth had gone dry. They were both right, but I didn't need to see his face. I'd have recognized that bind rune tattoo on his left shoulder from a mile away. One look at that familiar, simple black symbol unlocked a memory from a couple of years ago.

"I had a health scare when I was in my twenties," Cory

had told me while we'd cooled down after a workout. *"My grandfather—he believed runes were powerful, and after we knew everything was fine, he suggested getting this one. For health and vitality."* His soft smile had made my pulse jump. *"He got one with me."*

"You made sure the artist wasn't a trickster, right?" I'd asked, fighting the almost irresistible urge to run my fingers over the smooth lines.

"Are you kidding?" He'd scoffed. *"You think I'm going to risk Loki himself doing my tattoo?"* He shook his head. *"God, no. I went to a non-magic artist. I'm not stupid."*

No, he wasn't. I was, though. I'd made a deal with the fae, and that deal had me slamming face-first into my attraction to him at every turn.

Attraction. Right. Because that was clearly all this was.

I shook that thought away. Curiosity and maybe a smidge of masochism had me scrolling through his profile and everything he'd written. Not just reading the words, but hearing his voice in my ear as if Cory were sitting beside me and whispering all his desires right to me.

"I'm a top," I could hear him saying in a sultry purr. *"Also I won't be mad if you want to make out instead of watching the movie."*

It took all I had not to groan with frustration. I was never going to be able to concentrate on another movie in Cory's presence again. He liked to make out instead of watching? Really? Fuuuck. And of *course* he was a top. Of course he was. I'd known that for a long time. But the reminder didn't do much for maintaining my sanity.

And the profile went on.

"I don't mind hookups or friends with benefits. If there's potential for more, I'll probably take a while to warm up to an actual relationship—once bitten—but if you're patient

with me, we could really be something. If not, we can still have some fun."

I closed my eyes and exhaled. It was heartbreaking how cautious Cory was when it came to love. I didn't blame him, either—his last two exes had been real pieces of work, and I was pretty sure everyone in our social circle had celebrated when they'd gone. Cory had joined in with the first one; good riddance to bad rubbish and all that. The second... Well, he'd been utterly crushed. We'd all done what we could to support him and help him get through it, all the while quietly wishing the doors *had* hit that asshole on his way out. After how he'd treated Cory, after how he'd left him, that fucking dickhole deserved to be miserable like someone who'd crossed a fae.

"Would it be wrong to tell one of the fae that Max insulted their family?" Kayla had asked after one party where Cory had been a shell of himself. *"Put him on their collective shitlist?"*

"Absolutely not," I'd said through gritted teeth. *"But if the fae find out we lied..."* I'd grimaced. So had she.

So we hadn't gone to the fae and put the ex in the crosshairs of a trickster's grudge. It had sure been satisfying to imagine it, though.

"Well?" Andras prodded, smacking the side of my neck with his tail. "Are you going to swipe right on him or not?"

Sighing, I exited the profile without swiping either way. Then I closed the app, tossed my phone on the table, and got up. "I should get ready. Apparently I'm going clubbing tonight."

"But... but..." Raziel sputtered. "What about that profile? He's perfect!"

I winced. Oh yeah, he was absolutely perfect. He was also perfectly out of my reach, perfectly uninterested in anything beyond friendship with me—perfect for someone who wasn't me. He liked to let things progress slowly? Okay, I could buy that, but we'd known each other a long time. We were about as close as two people could be without crossing over into intimate territory. If it was going to happen, it would've happened a long time ago, so... no point in agonizing over it.

"I need to get ready" was all I said to Raziel and Andras.

They kept arguing, of course. With me. With each other. With my absolute idiocy at not swiping right on someone who was clearly put on this earth for the express purpose of being my exact match.

I just ignored them as best I could, which was surprisingly easy. All my whirring thoughts were louder than my annoying angel and demon. As I put on the khaki Henley Cory had picked out for me, a ball of lead grew in the pit of my stomach.

Could I really do this?

Not the part about going to a night club and dancing like I hadn't done since law school. I mean, yeah, I was still dubious of that. But...

Going with Cory?

How was I even supposed to notice other men with him in the room?

How was I supposed to connect with another man when the one I wanted more than any of them was *right there?*

This was going to be a nightmare.

I didn't even understand why I'd been such a wreck over Cory lately. I'd wanted him for ages, but I'd mostly made peace with us just being friends. Sure, there were nights when I thought about him in ways that would mortify him, and there were times when I wished I could put an arm around him, or more. But I knew where the lines were. I'd accepted them.

Until this past week.

I didn't even think it was just gratitude because he hadn't hesitated to help me with my current situation. There was just something about looking at my wants and needs and loneliness through a microscope with him that had all those desires surging to the surface. More than I ever had since I'd known him, I had to fight the impulse to look at him and say, *"Forget them—I want you."*

It was the loneliness talking. The loneliness, and also the desperation that came with being tangled up with the fae. Someday, years from now, we'd both be settled down with our partners. We'd have movie nights and dinners and hang out as four instead of two, and everyone would be content. Once in a while, I might look at him and think back on how I'd once pined for him, and then I'd smile and hold my partner closer and be grateful things had worked out the way they had.

Why did that seem about as likely as me stumbling into Mr. Right tonight?

For all I'd been mentally unraveling about going to the club tonight, I had overlooked one small detail:

That Cory would be *dressing* for a night out as well.

Now here he was, standing out on the curb beside me as we waited for our Uber. I could almost hear Andras wolf-whistling and commenting on how sexy Cory was, just as I could imagine Raziel delightedly detailing what a good-looking catch he was. Thank God the two of them had vanished into the ether, as per our agreement with their boss, so I had nothing to actually hear except for my own pounding heart.

Beside me, Cory had also gone for something simple. Tight black pants with a simple belt. A painted-on gray shirt. An unbuttoned black shirt over the top of that. Another pair of Chuck Taylors—bright blue this time.

I'd been reluctant to agree with pairing Chuck Taylors with what I was wearing, but Cory had insisted it would work. Now that I was looking at him... Okay. Yeah. I believed him. Glancing down at the black pair I was wearing, I just hoped I pulled off this aesthetic half as well as he did.

How am I supposed to even notice other men exist when you look that hot?

Our Uber arrived, and we slid into the backseat. As she pulled away from the curb, I turned to Cory. "Are you sure about this?"

He grinned. "Of course! It'll be fun!" He patted my thigh. "Trust me. Once you get there and have a drink to loosen up your nerves, you'll have a good time." With a wink, he added, "Just check out the scenery when we get there."

I remained skeptical. Didn't have much to say to argue, though, mostly because of that cool place on my leg where his hand had been. Words? What were words?

We didn't talk much on the way to the club. Fortunately, it was only about a fifteen-minute drive, and before I knew it, we were inside, and—

Oh. Fuck.

Flickering lights. Blasting music. Moving bodies. One step into this place, and my senses were overwhelmed. I didn't even know what to do. Where to start. Where to look. Where to go.

Cory was in his element, though, and he took my elbow and guided me to the bar. A couple of cocktails later —no idea what they were, though they tasted pretty good— we were at a table near the edge of the dancefloor, hunched over our drinks and peering at our surroundings. He'd assured me the alcohol would settle my nerves, and maybe it did a little. Or maybe I was just getting over the initial assault on my senses. Either way, I felt less like I was going to jump out of my skin. It was an improvement. I'd take it.

Cory leaned in and asked me something, but his words were lost in the warmth of his body and his soft breath grazing my skin. Good thing it was loud as hell, so pretending I just didn't hear him wouldn't rouse any suspicion.

Inching even closer, raising his voice a bit more, he managed to break through the fog: "See anything you like?"

Oh, I did. There were dozens of gorgeous men here, drinking and dancing and socializing and clearly out on the prowl. My gaze had landed on quite a few nice asses, pretty faces, and at least one guy who had his sleeves rolled to the elbows, revealing tatted up forearms.

And every last one of them blurred into the background like faceless extras in a movie. There may as well have been a spotlight right over Cory, picking out the coppery high-lights in his hair and the adorable, familiar sparkle in his dark eyes.

I cleared my throat and reached for my drink. "Y-yeah. There's..." I looked around, pretending to be checking out our surroundings and not just trying to take my gaze off him for a second. "A lot of options." I steeled myself and faced him again, plastering on a smile. "What about you?"

"Oh. Uh." He shifted a little and took a deep swallow

from his drink as he, too, scanned the room. "Yeah. A lot of good-looking guys out tonight."

I studied him. I knew why I wasn't thrilled to be here. Where had *his* enthusiasm gone?

Cory shook himself, smiled, and turned back toward me. "So. You gonna ask anyone to dance?"

"Ask—" I almost choked on the word. "I... God, no. I've never been good at approaching guys in a place like..." I gestured around us.

I half-expected him to admonish me and tell me to just put my dumb ass out there.

Instead, he shrugged. "Eh, I don't blame you. I'm terrible at it, too." Then he gave me a little down-up, winked, and added, "Pretty sure you won't have any trouble attracting someone who *will* ask."

My mouth instantly went dry. "You don't think so?"

"Uh, no." His laugh was quiet enough to be swallowed up by the noise around us, and he went for his drink again. "I don't think that'll be a problem."

I couldn't decide if it was the ever-changing lights or shadows, or if a few odd emotions really did flicker across his face. Emotions that didn't seem like they belonged here while he played wingman for a longtime friend. But nothing —the lights, the feelings—stayed still long enough for me to parse any of them.

I pulled my gaze away from him and out to the dance-floor. There was no point in sitting here pining after Cory. I was here for a reason, and the echoes of Andras and Raziel's voices in my ears kept me focused—mostly—on that reason.

Cory leaned in again. "What about him?" He nodded toward someone on the dancefloor.

"Which one?"

"Red shirt."

I searched the crowd, then found the red shirt and zeroed in on the guy. "Hmm. He's... not bad?"

"Not bad." Cory tsked and smacked my arm. "He looks like he could bench press both of us without breaking a sweat."

I laughed. "Or win a bodybuilder competition."

"Exactly."

I watched the guy for a moment, checking him out as he danced alone in the crowd. He wasn't hard on the eyes, that was for sure. He was, however, easily over a decade younger than me. Either he had a spectacular skincare routine, or his twenties weren't very far in the rearview.

I dropped my gaze into my drink. "He's a little young for me, I think."

"Ugh. Fine." Cory paused. "What about him?" He directed my attention to someone standing at the outskirts of a small group who all seemed to know each other. Very much on the prowl, judging by the way he kept checking out everyone else, but here with friends.

I gave him an appraising look, then shook my head. "I think I saw him on Grindr."

Cory raised his eyebrows. "Yeah?"

"Yeah. I think—oh, yeah. It was definitely him." I sipped my drink. "I swiped left."

Cory didn't ask me to elaborate. Instead, he continued searching the crowd for someone else who might pique my interest.

As if that was going to happen while he was here.

Right then, someone emerged from the crowd and appeared beside our table. He glanced at me, but quickly focused on Cory. "Hi." His grin was sharky, and his eyes were a beautiful blue that would've made me lose my breath if they were directed that intently on me.

Cory swallowed, but he smiled brightly. "Hi."

"Am I, uh..." The guy gestured at the two of us. "Interrupting anything?"

"No, no." Cory laughed and squeezed my arm. "We're just friends."

The way that man's eyes lit up made my heart sink. As the two of them chatted, I kept looking around the room. I didn't feel like a third wheel, really. This was why we'd both come here—the best-case scenario was both of us meeting someone before the end of the night. I just wasn't sure how much longer I could sit here and listen to someone flirting with Cory.

Fortunately, I didn't have to listen to it for very long.

Unfortunately, that was because now they were heading to the dancefloor.

Together.

And damn, dancing together, they were hot. The way they moved...

Who was I kidding? The way *he* moved. Cory could seriously dance, and he was dancing so damn close to that guy who was clearly interested in him. Who'd approached us, not knowing for sure whether we were a couple—who'd taken a risk because it was worth it for a chance at Cory.

They were going home together tonight. I just... I couldn't see this ending any other way.

Sitting there now, watching the chemistry spark between them, I was suddenly hit with years of regret. Why hadn't I ever made a move? Why hadn't I at least tried? Cory and I were friends. If he knew I was attracted to him, but he didn't return that attraction, it might be awkward for a little while, but we could weather it. And maybe that awkwardness would be worth it.

It couldn't be any worse than this crushing regret. This

white-hot anger at myself for being too much of a coward. This resignation because *something* might have been, but I'd been too scared to find out.

They'd just met, though. They were a song and a half into whatever might happen between them. Plenty of time for it to fizzle out or go awry, though I hoped for Cory's sake it didn't. I wasn't so sure I could handle watching his heart break again.

But it wasn't fizzling tonight. Not with the way they were holding each other close, talking to each other over the music and almost—almost—kissing.

If it does *fizzle tonight,* I promised myself, *I'm shooting my shot.*

Resignation suddenly melted away, leaving nothing but determination behind. No, I would never sabotage anything for Cory. But if this connection he had with this stranger didn't last the night...

Then I was going to find the courage to make that move.

CHAPTER 11

CORY

Eric was hot. Definitely. He had a smile that made my knees weak, and those eyes—my God. I even wondered if he might be a magic user; eyes that beautiful *had* to be the result of sorcery.

But asking meant speaking, and I wasn't so great for that right now. With his hands on my hips and our bodies this close together, I was lucky I could breathe. My heart was going wild, and every time he tilted his head like he might move in and kiss me, I almost melted. When he licked his lips... oh, God. So hot.

And yet...

I felt...

Nothing.

Yeah, there were physical reactions. He gave me goose bumps and made breath hard to come by. He made my pulse race and my legs unsteady.

But beneath all that was an emotional flatline.

I didn't need to be in love with someone to sleep with them. I had plenty of casual sex, and the whole friends-with-benefits thing was totally fine with me. But this wasn't just a lack of a connection to Eric. It was... something *missing*. In me. A void that was somehow both empty and heavy.

What is wrong with me tonight?

Ugh. Who was I kidding? There was only one man in this club who was going to provoke more than a physical reaction from me, and he wasn't on this dancefloor.

Suddenly I didn't want to be either.

I slowed my steps and sighed. Eric's smile vanished in favor of concern, which made me feel even worse about backing away from him. He seemed like a nice guy. Which also meant he deserved someone who was way more engaged than I was, even if he was just looking for a hookup.

"I, um..." I shook my head, avoiding his eyes. "I'm not sure I'm..."

"Hey. It's okay." He gave my arm a little squeeze and stepped back, giving me some breathing room. "If you're not into it, you're not into it."

I met his gaze again. God, he really was a nice guy. I'd met plenty of dudes who'd cop an attitude or turn into Mr. Hyde at a moment like this, but aside from some unmistakable disappointment, there was only concern in his expression.

"I'm sorry," I said.

"Nothing to be sorry about." He squeezed my arm again. Then he vanished like a mirage into the crowd.

A surge of regret tried to send me after him, but I knew it was pointless. My heart wasn't in it tonight. End of story.

What I needed in that moment was a drink.

I was almost to the edge of the floor when a hand gently caught my elbow. I turned, readying an apologetic rejection... and froze.

"You're not done dancing, are you?" Matt's grin made my knees shake.

I swept my tongue across my suddenly parched lips. Shouting over the music, I stammered, "I... Um... That depends."

His eyebrows rose.

I swallowed. "If I stay, am I dancing with you?"

The grin broadened, and he tugged my arm. What could I do but follow?

Oh. Fuck. Was this... Was this really happening?

Yeah, it was. Matt's hands were on me. His body was against mine. We were moving. He was looking at me. And...

Holy shit. This is real.

It was too loud to talk. That was probably a good thing, because dozens of questions were ricocheting around in my skull. Most of them boiled down to... *why?*

Why were we dancing? Why was he looking at me that way? Why did his hands fit so perfectly on my waist? Why...

Why had it taken us so long to do this?

And why were we dancing closer...

Closer...

Holy fuck, he was so close.

"Matt..." I didn't even know what I wanted to say. What thought there was to finish. Looking in his eyes from this close up, I couldn't think at all. Especially not while he was looking right back at me. We were surrounded by hot guys. Guys who wouldn't be out of place in an underwear ad or on the cover of a magazine. Guys with so much more to offer than me.

But Matt...

Was looking...

At me.

That empty, heavy void behind my ribs was such a distant memory now, it was weird to imagine it had ever been there at all. Not when there was this fire. This heat. This *need*.

I didn't even know what my feet were doing anymore. I'd lost all sense of rhythm. Couldn't separate the thumping bass from my pounding heart. Couldn't catch my damn breath without tasting Matt's cologne.

And if the space between us narrowed even a sliver, he was going to notice exactly what he was doing to me.

His eyes flicked to my lips, and I swear to God, the hunger blazing in his expression almost made me come right there on the dancefloor.

Fuck it. I slid my hands up his back and leaned in closer, and I felt more than heard the growl he released as my hard-on brushed his, and even though I'd been the one to move in, the moment our lips touched, it was *him* claiming *me*. I melted against him, knees unsteady, and somewhere in between him stealing my breath and deepening that kiss, my mind swerved back to that thick ridge pressing against my groin. I'd felt it, known he was hard, but it had taken a few seconds to catch up and realize... *he was hard*. He was turned on.

Oh, God. Matt wanted this. Wanted *me*.

I pushed my hands into his back pockets as I kissed him harder. The deafening music swallowed the sound of his voice, but the thrum of his low groan reverberated through me like the bass thumping around us. His mouth was needy and hungry, and I was just... putty. We weren't even dancing anymore, and I didn't give a damn. Not as long as he was kissing me and sliding those amazing hands all over me. I wanted him so—

Someone bumped into us. Then another.

"We should..." I tipped my head toward the edge of the dancefloor.

Matt nodded, and we made our way through the crowd. As soon as we were clear of it, I spun around, grabbed him, and pulled him to me. He pushed me up against the wall, and oh, fuck, this was the sexiest thing I'd ever experienced. Matt's kiss was deep and needy. His hands under my over-shirt were hot, his fingers digging in as if he needed me as close to his body as possible.

No one had ever kissed me like this before. *No one.* Like he was overcome with an all-consuming need to have me. With a lot of guys, being pinned like this—being held against a wall—would have some claustrophobia worming its way through my arousal, but not this time. Matt was safe. Everything about this was hot and demanding and reckless and *safe*.

Because this was Matt.

Holy shit. This was what it felt like to kiss Matt. To be in Matt's arms. To be pinned and held and irresistibly *craved* by *Matt*.

And that was to say nothing about how dizzying it was to have his hard-on rutting against mine. Something about knowing this was Matt—that *he* was the one who was rock-hard for me—had me almost delirious with want. I wasn't usually one to get so turned on I came in my pants after some frotting and making out, but there was a first time for everything, and if he kept this up...

Matt broke the kiss, and I sucked in air... then forgot how to breathe because his lips were on my neck, skating up and down the side of my throat as his hands slid between my back and the wall.

He kissed under my ear and murmured just loud

enough for me and no one else to hear, "Any chance you want to get out of here?"

Get out of... Oh. Right. We were still in the club, weren't we? Still in public and in our clothes.

And we'd only started dancing, like, two minutes ago? Right? Wasn't this a little fast?

I've also wanted him for five goddamned years. Fast, my ass.

I nodded as I tried to catch my breath. "Y-yeah. Let's... I'll get us an Uber."

That was the plan, anyway.

As we stumbled out onto the sidewalk, the club's music still ringing in my ears and thumping in the air, I took out my phone. Just needed to open the Uber app, request a—

"Uh, Cory?" Matt sounded confused and a bit alarmed.

I looked up.

And just like that the music was gone.

So was the other bar across the street. In its place was the Italian restaurant where we frequently grabbed takeout and that one cashier always flirted with me.

I turned around slowly.

No club. No neon lights. No bouncer. No line outside.

Just our apartment building.

All around us, the familiar night noises settled in. A TV on too loud coming through an open window. The engine of a passing car a couple streets over. A distant siren.

"Am I..." Matt cleared his throat. "Am I hallucinating?"

I did a slow turn, taking in the street and buildings that had been home for the past few years. "If you are, then so am I."

My gaze landed on Matt. His eyes were wide, his expression almost comically full of the same *what the fuck?* I was feeling.

But then I realized... we were home.

I didn't care if we'd just put ourselves in debt to the fae until the end of time. This was one gift horse I had no interest in looking in the mouth for at least a couple of hours.

I took Matt's hand. "Who cares? We're home."

His focus sharpened, and the fire he'd had in the club returned. "Good call."

My apartment was on the first floor, so we went there without any discussion. It took me longer than I cared to admit to unlock the door, but once it came open, I tossed my keys somewhere in the vicinity of the couch and grabbed Matt's shirt. He kicked the door shut behind him, and this time it was my turn to pin him with a hungry, greedy kiss. I had enough presence of mind to turn the deadbolt. After that, nothing existed except Matt and all these clothes that needed to get the hell out of the way.

"As much as I love how this shirt looks on you," I mumbled between kisses, "it really, really needs to come off."

Matt responded with a soft moan. Then, "So what are you going to do about it?"

Oh, it was going to be like that?

All right, then.

I slid my hands under his shirt and pushed it up, all my senses going haywire as my palms ran along his hot body. He raised his arms, peeled the shirt the rest of the way off, and tossed it aside, and I had a split second to be satisfied that that Henley had in fact wound up in a crumpled heap on *my* floor. The second Matt's lips met mine again, I forgot all about any clothing except what we were both still wearing.

Matt pushed my button-up shirt over my shoulders, and

I shrugged it away. It snagged on my hand, and I shook it off like a spider web before putting my hand back on Matt's body where it belonged.

We got rid of my T-shirt. Then Matt nudged me back a step, and I got the message—we needed to be someplace more comfortable. Ideally someplace horizontal.

Fortunately, my apartment came equipped with just such a place, and oh my God, this had to be a dream. There was no way I was dragging Matt Russo down on top of me in my bed. No way we were making out. Rubbing clothed hard-ons together. Running hands all over bare skin. This wasn't possible. Finding ourselves transported here to our building was a hell of a lot more believable than Matt being here, half-naked and fully hard, groaning into my kiss and trembling with barely restrained need. Need for *me*.

I dragged my nails up his back, reveling in his shuddering moan.

He pushed himself up on his hands and gazed down at me, as out of breath as I was. "This is..." He licked his swollen lips. "This is not how I saw tonight playing out."

I laughed, sounding a bit drunk, and I teased his nipple with my thumbnail. "Same, but I have no complaints."

The little grin that flickered across his gorgeous mouth gave me more goose bumps. So did that kiss as he sank back down on top of me.

"I don't even know where to start," he murmured. "I just... God, I want you."

That was the closest I'd ever been to words almost sending me over the edge. My toes curled and my back arched, and by some miracle, I didn't actually lose it. Breathless and trembling, I said, "We could start by getting naked."

"Mmm, good idea," he growled, and then his kiss almost finished the job.

Getting his pants off didn't take much work, seeing as he preferred a more relaxed fit. The snug-ass *please-check-out-my-butt-and-package, gentlemen* pants I was wearing? Well, that was neither easy nor graceful, but in the end, they were on the floor with his clothes. Perfect.

"Ooh," he purred as he closed his fingers around my erection. "You're packing even more than I thought."

Some snarky part of me wanted to ask just how much he'd thought about what I was packing, but that part short-circuited into silence because oh, fuck, this man's hands were talented. His strokes were slow and perfect, driving me absolutely out of my mind.

I still had some synapses firing, though. Particularly the ones involved in thinking I should reciprocate, and also that I wanted my hands on him, too. He was hardly lacking, either, but what had my pulse soaring was the way my first stroke made him close his eyes and swear. God, I could get lost in watching his hunger and arousal play out on his face. The lip bites. How he'd squeeze his eyes shut, or how they'd fly open when he gasped and shivered. The subtle flush in his fair skin. Even the magic he was working on my dick couldn't pull my attention away from how sexy and responsive he was.

"Jesus Christ," he murmured, thrusting into my hand as he pumped my cock. "I can't decide if I want to spend the whole night doing everything, or if I just want you to fuck me until I cry."

My own strokes faltered. I couldn't decide either. Exploring every inch of him and savoring this man I'd never imagined touching? Or pounding him into the mattress? All those times I'd heard him through the ceiling—was I really about to hear all that up close? Was I really about to drive those delicious sounds out of him?

I squirmed on the mattress. "I think I'm too keyed up to take it slow."

Matt's eyes sparked with both surprise and interest. "Yeah?"

"Uh-huh." I licked my lips. "You game?"

The gleam in those eyes answered before his mouth did, and when he spoke, his voice came out hoarse with need: "Fuck taking it slow."

I grinned as goose bumps sprang up all over my spine. "Let me get a condom."

CHAPTER 12

MATT

I was going to come absolutely unraveled.

Just watching Cory rolling on the condom with unsteady hands had my heart pounding and my mind racing. I still couldn't get my head around everything that had happened at the club. That I'd watched him walk away from that other guy and somehow—from some reserve I'd probably never find again—conjured up the courage to ask Cory to dance. And dancing had turned into...

I shivered. That first kiss had been unreal. I'd always loved kissing, but no one had ever stopped my world on a dime like Cory had the moment our lips had touched. All this time, wondering what his mouth would taste like, what his body would feel like, and now it was real.

"Christ," he muttered as he finally got the condom to cooperate. "These things are too complicated when I'm this turned on."

I laughed, almost delirious with need and arousal and a million things I'd never felt before. Not even in those early days with the man I'd intended to spend the rest of my life with.

As Cory came closer, probably about to ask me how I wanted it, I cupped his neck and claimed another kiss. He didn't protest. A soft moan vibrated against my lips, and then we were sinking down to the bed, naked and tangled up in each other. I wanted—*needed*—him balls deep in me, but I couldn't get enough of his perfect kiss.

It was Cory who broke that kiss, panting hard as he touched his forehead to mine. "I did... I did all that work getting the condom on." He brushed our lips together. "Shouldn't let it go to waste."

I laughed. "Is that a roundabout way of saying you want to fuck?"

"How about you turn around so we can fuck?"

I shivered, which made him grin, and we stole another long kiss before I did as he'd asked while he reached for the lube. He made short work of prepping me—not rushing it, but not taking all goddamned night either. I wasn't sure either of us could wait much longer.

And then...

"Oh, fuck." I almost choked on my own voice as he pushed into me. "God, yeah..."

He made a sound that was halfway between a laugh and a moan. As if he were amused and smug, but also so turned on he could barely breathe. Having that effect on him? On *Cory*? Oh, hell, that was hot.

Adjusting his grasp on my hips, he murmured, "Like that?"

I managed something in the neighborhood of "fuck yes," and his chuckle was full of smugness. He deserved to be smug, I supposed. If I had a dick that could turn a man to an inarticulate mess like this, I'd be smug as hell, too.

For all he'd promised this would be quick, though, that he was too keyed up to take it slow or easy, he was in no hurry now that he was inside me. His strokes were long and languid, scrambling my thoughts with a delirious mix of pleasure and frustration.

I tried rocking my hips, but he held them still, his grip surprisingly strong.

"What's the matter?" he teased. "Don't you like this?"

"I do. It's... God. Cory." I let my head fall forward as a shudder ran through me. *"Harder."*

The low groan he released was too sexy for words, but I only had a heartbeat or two to savor it because oh, fuck, he gave it to me harder. He was thicker than I was used to, and the intensity—the ecstasy—had my eyes watering as I gripped handfuls of his sheets and pleaded for more, more, more.

"Oh, fuck," he panted, driving painfully into me as he held my hips in an iron grip. "You're so damn..." He shuddered hard, making him gasp and throwing off his rhythm for half a stroke before he recovered and continued slamming into me like his life depended on it. "Christ, Matt. You're *perfect.*"

I bit my lip and tried not to lose my mind. Quick was fine and good, but for all I wasn't sure I could handle another second of this pure, intense bliss, I wasn't ready for this to be over. Just a little more... A few more thrusts... A few more squeaks of his bed to punctuate his ragged curses...

Then he shouted something I was too far gone to understand, thrust into me hard enough to knock me down onto my forearms, and trembled all over with the force of his orgasm.

As fast as my head was spinning... As hard as it was to hold on to a single thought... I might as well have been coming, too. But no, I wasn't. Holy hell. Would I survive an orgasm from this man? Something told me I was about to find out.

Cory eased his grip on my hips. With a sigh, he pulled out, and his voice was slurred as he said, "Gonna get rid of this. Back in a sec."

I murmured an affirmative and nodded.

The mattress dipped, and I sensed him leaving the room. I rolled onto my back and gave myself a few slow, lazy pulls just to keep myself from going out of my mind from arousal.

Cory returned a moment later, his eyes heavy-lidded and still full of fire. He looked me up and down, pressed his shoulder against the doorframe, and grinned. "Ooh, maybe I should just stay back here and watch."

"Don't you dare," I rasped, still stroking myself.

An eyebrow flicked up as he crossed his arms. "Or what? You're either going to keep touching yourself or not. Either way..." He made a big gesture of raking his eyes over me. "I get a hell of a view."

My back arched as my toes curled, and I growled, "Get over here."

For a few painfully long seconds, I was sure he was going to make good on that threat to stand there and watch. Mercifully, he pushed himself off the doorframe, crossed the room, crawled up the bed, and—

"Oh. Fuuuck..." The magic he worked with his mouth would've made sorcerers weep. He had me arching and writhing, almost levitating off his bed, with nothing more than the slide of his lips and the soft flutters of his tongue. He didn't miss an inch—from the head all the way down and over my balls—and that was before he pushed a couple of fingers into me. When his mouth and hand found a rhythm, I forgot how to breathe. Forgot how to think. Forgot how to do anything except lie there and be completely at his mercy.

It didn't take him long at all to bring me to the edge, and once he had me there, he held me there, kept me there, teasing and licking and fingering me just to—but not beyond —that brink.

"Cory..." I pleaded, almost sobbing with need. "Please..."

He hummed around my dick, and then... Then he did something. With his tongue? His fingers? Both at the same time?

Whatever it was, the edge was suddenly a distant memory, and my hips bucked like they had a mind of their own as I tried to push deeper into his eager mouth, my orgasm turning everything bright white.

With a shudder and a few curses, I sank back to the bed. I wasn't just trembling all over—I was vibrating, every nerve in my body alight with electric pleasure.

"Oh, fuck..." I murmured.

Cory laughed softly, and I gasped as he slipped his fingers free. Then he was over me again, his mouth on mine, and the whole room spun around us as we kissed while I slowly returned to earth.

After I didn't know how long, I broke the kiss and met his gaze. I combed shaky fingers through his tousled hair. How was this real? How was Cory touching me like this and looking at me like that?

A smile flickered across his lips. Then he leaned down and...

God. How was Cory *kissing* me like this? On the heels of sex that amazing? I wasn't dead, was I?

No, I was pretty sure I wasn't dead. But I still couldn't believe this was real.

Slowly, though, as we lazily made out, the dust settled and smoke cleared.

And as they did, a cold ball of lead swelled beneath my ribs.

This *was* real. And I suddenly wasn't so sure it should've been.

What had we just done?

Yeah, it was hot, and no, I'd never been averse to jumping into bed with someone. But was this really what I wanted *with Cory?* We were friends. What if sex screwed that up? Especially since there'd been a moment or two where it had felt dangerously close to making love, and I was terrified that had been one-sided. That this had just been sex for Cory.

I had no idea where I stood with him now. No idea where this would leave us. We needed to have a conversation now, and I was suddenly afraid that conversation would end with him farther out of my reach than he'd been before.

What if the most amazing sex I've ever had was just a hookup for him?

Shit. We should've talked beforehand. At least made sure we were on the same page about what this was and what it wasn't.

What if we want different things, and the air between us gets weird now?

Damn it. I needed to go. I wanted to be here more than anywhere else in the world, but I needed to get as far away from here as I could so I could gather my thoughts and figure out how to do damage control. I needed to think, and I couldn't think while I was naked in Cory's arms.

What if we—

A familiar crackle of electricity had my eyes flying open,

and I jumped a split second before Andras appeared on my shoulder. A glance around, and I found Raziel hovering between us above the pillows.

I scrambled up and pulled the sheet up to my waist. "What the fuck? What are you guys—what the fuck?"

Cory also sat up, his eyes wide and cheeks red as he, too, covered himself. He swallowed, gaze flicking back and forth between Andras and Raziel. When he met my eyes, confusion filled his expression, but there was something else, too. Something more raw. Hurt? Then he spoke, and yeah, there was some pain there: "What's going on?"

I shook my head. "I have no idea. I thought..." I peered at Andras. "I thought you two were supposed to be gone after I..." I gestured at Cory and myself. Cory's lips thinned, the hurt in his expression shifting to something frostier and more closed off.

"We're here to find you a companion," Raziel said cheerfully, oblivious to the air turning weird between Cory and me. "Our work isn't done!"

"But you said..." I shook myself. "You said you were here to get me laid."

"And find you a companion." Andras gave a derisive snort. "Does *anyone* around here read the briefings? Or at least the fecking contract you signed?"

"But isn't..." I stared at him. Then at Raziel. Then at Cory.

And my heart sank.

Oh. Well. I guess that settled that. Good thing I hadn't gotten around to spilling my guts to Cory and telling him I wanted something more, because if Andras and Raziel were here, then...

Then I guess I had my answer.

But then I realized that all the heat in Cory's expression

—all the warmth, the affection, the hunger—was gone, though I couldn't decide if he looked ready to break or ready to lose his temper. Maybe both.

Wait. Was I misreading the moment?

I opened my mouth to speak, but he was faster.

"Maybe we should call it a night," he said flatly. His eyes pleaded with me to read between the lines: *I need you to go. Now.*

Oh, fuck. I didn't even know where to start to do damage control right now, and I sure as shit couldn't do it with Andras and Raziel literally looking over my shoulders. I'd already been mentally reeling from everything we'd done tonight. Already trying to process how we'd made it into his bed and where the hell we went from here.

Now the only place he wanted me to go was *out.*

Okay. Okay, we could step away and catch our breath. Somehow, I could figure out how to do some goddamned damage control, but not until Cory could handle being in the same room with me.

Neither of us said a word as I found what clothes had made it into his bedroom. I dressed, murmured that we'd talk soon, and headed out, intending to pick up my remaining clothing and then get the hell up to my own apartment.

I almost had my hand on the bedroom doorknob when his voice halted me in my tracks.

"Matt."

Though I wasn't sure I could face him again tonight, I turned. And goddammit, the hurt in his eyes was too damn much.

So was the shakiness in his voice as he said, "I want to help you get rid of them. I do. But I can't..."

I lowered my gaze as shame knotted in my stomach. "I know. I'm sorry. I—"

"If anyone can break the spell, it's the Trickster King." Cory's voice sounded close to cracking. "And he owes me a favor."

I locked eyes with him again. "You'd... let me use..."

He was the one to look away this time, but not fast enough to hide the shimmer above his lower lashes. "Yeah. Just, um... Just let me know."

That shame wound even tighter. Galen didn't give out favors to just anyone, and no one in their right mind would piss away one he had on reserve. But I didn't think this was just Cory being the most amazing friend I could ask for—he was doing this for himself, too. Because he wouldn't abandon me to the consequences of this stupid spell—that wasn't who he was—but he also couldn't stand another minute of helping me. Not after everything we'd done. Everything I'd asked of him. Everything I'd taken from him.

Escaping the heartache I was bringing him was worth letting go of a favor from the Trickster King.

I swallowed hard, my own voice shaky. "I can't take—"

"I can't take another minute of this," he shot back, facing me with the full force of his pain in those tear-filled eyes. "I'd rather lose that favor than lose my friend, and after tonight..." He closed his eyes and wiped at them.

I didn't push him to elaborate. It was clear enough—after tonight, we'd strained our friendship to its breaking point, and despite no doubt being angry and hurt and wishing I'd just *leave* already, he was willing to give up whatever he could to keep us from pushing past that point.

I suddenly couldn't stay here a second longer. The post-sex awkwardness had nothing on this, and I couldn't take it.

I suspected he wanted me gone, too, so I cleared my throat. "We'll talk in the morning."

Then I left.

By some miracle, I didn't forget to grab my remaining clothes. Somehow, I found my keys, too, and I remembered which one would let me into my apartment.

Raziel started to say something on the way up the stairs, but I put up a hand. "No. I don't want to hear another word tonight."

He sputtered in protest. Andras sighed and told him, "Leave him be, Razi."

"But—"

"Let the man sleep."

As if sleep was going to happen any time soon, but at least the two of them were silent after that.

Mere minutes after I'd been wrapped up in Cory's amazing arms in his rumpled bed…

I was home.

And even with the silent angel and demon on my shoulders…

I was more alone than I'd been before I'd had dinner with Bridget.

CHAPTER 13

CORY

Nothing I'd ever experienced came close to the ecstasy of sex with Matt.

And nothing came anywhere near the crushing hurt of realizing Andras and Raziel were back. What that meant.

Fuck. *Really*, Matt?

Yeah. Really. Because apparently in all the chaos and confusion, Matt—Matthew A. Russo, Esquire, ever the thorough and detail-oriented lawyer—had missed the part where Andras was just being crass about getting him laid. That was the only explanation I could land on. Because he'd thought getting dicked down would do the trick, but no, they'd been here to find him a *companion*. More than a warm body with a hard cock. More than a hookup.

More than whatever he'd wanted from me last night.

Christ. Who knew I could actually feel *worse* than I had when I'd wished Matt knew I was into him?

I muttered some curses as I rolled out of my otherwise empty bed and onto my feet. I was exhausted and drained like I'd never been before—so emotionally wrung out I could barely move—but I suddenly needed to take the hottest shower I could stand. I felt disgusting. The sex had been amazing, but now that Matt was gone...

How could I be so stupid?

That was easy enough—because I *was* stupid when it came to Matt. He was everything I wanted in a man, and for him, I'd been a means to an end. One that hadn't even worked.

Letting the hot spray run over my back and shoulders, I rubbed my eyes and sighed. Maybe I should be grateful Andras and Raziel had been there. They'd been a bucket of ice water over an otherwise amazing moment, but they'd been a bucket of cold hard *truth*. They'd shown themselves, and in doing so, they'd shown Matt for what he was.

Could I even be angry at him? If I'd had those two following me around, not to mention the clock ticking down on a very brief window of time when they wouldn't *always* be following me around, I'd have done desperate shit, too.

I just hadn't imagined I'd be the thing Matt would do out of desperation.

My eyes stung. Why did I care if I cried? It wasn't like anyone was going to see or hear me.

Probably because I hated this feeling, and I hated letting it crash over me the way it was so determined to do. But I was too exhausted and crushed to fight it, so... I didn't.

I braced a hand against the cold wall to keep my balance, and I let the dam break. Let myself feel the hurt of knowing—not just suspecting, but *knowing*—that Matt was out of my league. Let that amazing sex replay in my mind alongside the reality that it hadn't been anything to him. Nothing except an orgasm and—he'd hoped—what he needed to break a curse.

Where the fuck did all that leave me?

It doesn't matter to Matt.

That hit me in the chest. No, I didn't know where this left me, but the fact that it didn't matter to him... That he'd happily used me to try to get out of the agreement his dumb ass had made with the fae...

I kind of wanted to rescind my offer to let him use my favor from the Trickster King, but... no. No, I couldn't do that, and I wouldn't.

Because fuck me, but no matter what Matt did, no matter how little he cared about me...

I still loved him.

I'd still do any goddamned thing for him.

I squeezed my eyes shut as more hot tears slid free.

Would you even care if you knew what you were doing to me, Matt?

In that moment, I was glad he'd left. I was relieved he wasn't here for me to ask.

Because I really didn't want to know.

CHAPTER 14

MATT

The maelstrom of emotions churning inside me had been too much to sort out. Between the sex and the heartache, I'd been exhausted, and I hadn't been able to think anymore.

I'd barely been able to speak, my voice so close to cracking as I told Andras and Raziel, "Just... leave me alone for the rest of the night, okay? I need to..."

Sleep? Think? Cry? Well, in the end, I did manage two of those things.

Now I was right where I'd been when this whole shit-show had started—staring at myself in my bathroom mirror, my jaw scruffy and my eyes bloodshot as I tried to comprehend the angel and demon perched on my shoulders.

It wasn't the same level of shock this time. And the red in my eyes had nothing to do with alcohol. The panic roiling in my chest wasn't the same either, but like last time, I couldn't figure out what to do with it.

My voice came out raw and brittle: "I don't understand. Why are you guys still here?"

From their respective perches, Andras and Raziel eyed me like I'd lost my mind.

"What do you mean?" Raziel asked. "We left while you were, as you put it"—he made air quotes—"'on the prowl,' and while you were, um..." He actually blushed, which would've been funny if I hadn't been this close to curling up on the floor and sobbing.

Andras rolled his eyes. "While he was getting railed up the arse by his neighbor?"

Raziel turned even redder.

I glared at Andras. "So you weren't there, but you know what I was doing."

He rolled his eyes again. "Well, I do now."

"For fuck's sake." I pressed a hand against the counter and wiped the other over my face. Dropping that hand to the counter, I glared at both of them in the mirror. "I just don't get it—why are you still here after last night?"

"Why wouldn't we be?" Raziel asked as if I'd just asked the stupidest question ever. "Our work isn't done."

"The hell it isn't!" I groaned. "You said you were here to get me laid. I got laid. So why..." I pointed at each of them. "Do I have to do a survey or some shit before you leave?"

"You think last night counts?" Andras scoffed. "If you just needed to help someone polish his knob, we'd have put you on Grindr the first night and got on with it."

I blinked. "But... we *did* put me on Grindr. And Tinder. And... It still doesn't matter. You said you were here to—"

"We're here to find you a companion," Raziel said.

"But *he* said you were here to—"

"My colleague has been known to oversimplify matters." Raziel shot Andras a look. Andras silently mocked his words.

I narrowed my eyes. "Oversimplify them, how?"

"Well." Raziel straightened a little and cleared his throat. "Carnal relations are certainly, well, if that's what you want—but it's not the whole deal. I said we were here to find you a *companion*." He huffed and sounded seriously smug as he added, "You read the agreement just like I read the briefing. You know the deal."

"Yeah, I did," I croaked.

Except... oh fuck. I hadn't. I'd been so fixated on and panicked over the visibility of Andras and Raziel, I'd overlooked... everything. The specifics of what qualified as a "companion" to break this spell. I was a fucking lawyer. I did this for a living. I... God, I was *so stupid*.

Except...

"I'm still confused. Last night *wasn't* just a hookup." I threw up my hands. "How the fuck doesn't it count when I spent the night with a man I've been in love with for years?"

Neither of the beings on my shoulders responded. They stared at me. I stared at them.

Then I met my own eyes in the mirror.

And my words echoed in my ears.

"How the fuck doesn't it count when I spent the night with a man I've been in love with for years?"

My shoulders drooped beneath Andras and Raziel, nearly unloading the former. "Because he doesn't feel the same way."

"Oh, for fuck's sake!" Andras snapped his wings, and this time he caught my ear, which stung. Unaware of or not caring about that part, he stomped on my collarbone and stared at me in the mirror, gesturing sharply at me. "Are you mad? Or just daft?"

I blinked. "What are you talking about?"

"You don't think he feels the same way?" Andras groaned, rolling his eyes. "Fucking hell, Razi. We should've been taking this man to an optician instead of shopping."

Raziel just nodded.

I stared at both of them. "What are you talking about? If he feels the same way, then why the fuck did you two show up and ruin the moment?"

The angel shrugged. "You were pulling away. We showed up to assist!"

"Assist?" I narrowed my eyes. "By making him think all I wanted from him was a hookup? Christ, I..."

I trailed off as I ran through where my thoughts had been in the moments before Andras and Raziel had appeared. I'd been panicking. Certain we'd royally fucked everything up. Ready to bail like a goddamned coward so I could have a moment to pull my thoughts together and...

And leave Cory alone while I figured myself out.

"Oh my God," I breathed, and hung my head. "I'm so fucking stupid."

"Now he gets it," Andras said.

I batted him off my shoulder, but even his indignant squawk wasn't enough to break through the dark cloud settling over me. "Why the fuck did you try to tell me before that sleeping with Cory would fix this?"

Andras sighed theatrically. "Because we thought once you idiots got into bed, you'd take it from there!" He threw up his hands again and snapped his wings. "But here we fucking are!"

Yeah. Here we fucking were. So damn stupid.

"So what now?" My voice sounded pathetic to my own ears as I whispered, "I don't know what to do. I just... I love him so damn much."

"Then tell him," Raziel prodded gently.

I squeezed my eyes shut, pretending they didn't sting. "He probably hates me after last night." Hell, I hated me after last night. I'd gone from having the most incredible sex ever to watching all that pain register on Cory's face as he'd realized—falsely—that it hadn't meant anything to me. That *he* hadn't meant anything.

"He's gonna rightfully hate you if you keep blubbering and feeling sorry for yourself," Andras said. "Get your arse down there and talk to him, you fucking numpty."

I half-expected Raziel to chastise him for the harsh comment or the language, but he didn't. When I met the angel's gaze in the mirror, his expression said nothing if not, *"Well? Why are you just standing here?"*

And... why *was* I just standing there?

Because every second Cory didn't know how I really felt was another second of him hurting and quite possibly hating me.

A surge of both panic and determination had me standing straighter. I needed to do this. Now. Right the hell now.

"You two, stay—" I thought fast. "Fifteen minutes. Give me fifteen minutes."

"As you wish," Raziel said.

Andras gave a flippant shrug.

Then they were both gone.

My pulse surged and I sprinted out of the bathroom.

And halfway down the hall, I darted back in to brush my teeth. If this went well, then I wasn't about to spoil it with morning breath.

With my mouth tasting a bit more pleasant, I once again hurried down the hall, then out of my apartment and down the stairs. I pounded on his door as frantically as I had the morning Andras and Raziel had first appeared. Maybe a little more frantically. Because somehow I was in an even bigger panic now than when I'd awakened to find a pair of winged weirdos on my shoulders.

Just as it had that first day, the deadbolt clicked and door opened.

Just as he had that first day, Cory met my gaze across the threshold.

But this time, his expression wasn't full of concern or worry.

No, those beautiful eyes were regarding me uneasily. Suspiciously, even. And when they flicked from my left shoulder to my right, some hurt crept in as he said, "Looks like you got rid of them." His smile was thin, hinting at more of the hurt in his eyes. "Glad I could help."

"No, I asked them to—I've only got fifteen minutes. Probably closer to ten now. But I—"

"The Trickster King favor. Right." He stood aside and gestured for me to come in. "Let me get the—"

"No! I'm not here for…" I paused to collect my thoughts. I didn't want to do this out here. If I humiliated myself, fine, but he didn't deserve to have our neighbors staring at us. Voice as calm as I could manage—and that didn't say much —I said, "I'm not coming to ask for anything from you. Just… can we talk?" I nodded past him. "Inside?"

The suspicion and hurt hung on tight, but curiosity pushed one eyebrow up ever so slightly. Swallowing hard, Cory stepped aside and gestured for me to come in.

And as soon as the door was shut and we had the privacy he deserved, I started talking, and I started talking fast.

"I'm sorry. I'm—I fucked up last night. And I don't mean by getting into bed with you."

Both eyebrows were up now.

I went on before I lost my momentum, "Everything— the club, in your bedroom—it was all perfect. It was amazing. I… I don't know why I freaked out. Or why I left.

Because to tell you the truth, I've been wishing for a long, long time that last night would happen."

Cory's lips parted. "You... Seriously?"

"Yes," I whispered. "And I think... I think when I realized we were there... That we'd slept together..." I shook my head and pushed out a breath. "I'm sorry. I don't know. I guess I was afraid you'd do exactly what I ended up doing."

He cocked his head. "What? Leaving?"

"Or, well, telling me to leave."

He stared at me like I'd spoken in another language. "Why would I do that?"

"Because you can do so much better than me." God, I sounded pathetic. "I know you've been frustrated being single, but I've been absolutely sure all this time that the right guy for you is going to show up any minute. Because holy shit, if there's anyone in this world who deserves to have the most amazing partner on the planet, it's you. And no matter how long I've been completely and stupidly in love with you, I can't imagine ever living up to that."

Once again, Cory watched me as if he hadn't understood a word I'd said. But before I could keep rambling, he softly asked, "You... You're in love with me?"

My chest ached, and my voice came out ragged: "Yes. How could I not be?" I raked a hand through my hair. "I mean... Hell. Dancing with you last night? Ending up back here? I think that was inevitable as soon as we walked in the door."

"How... How do you figure?"

My shoulders sagged. "Because you were the only man in that building who caught my attention. That's why I couldn't resist asking you to dance, because it wasn't like I noticed anyone else." I sighed, dropping my gaze. "And then afterward, I guess I freaked out. All this time, I didn't even want to let myself believe I was because there's no way in hell I'll ever be what—"

"Matt." Cory's voice was sharp enough to stop me mid-sentence. He held my gaze. Then he shook his head, stepped closer, and whispered, "Shut up," a second before he grabbed my neck and...

Kissed me.

My God. This was nothing like the way he'd kissed me last night. It was soft, and sweet, and stopped time. I wrapped my arms around him, both to hold him to me and to make sure he was real. That this wasn't some bizarre dream.

It was so, so real. So perfectly, earth-shakingly real.

When Cory's lips finally left mine, he still held me close, and we were both trembling and out of breath. I couldn't find my voice, never mind words, but he didn't have that problem.

"I almost married someone once," he said, voice as unsteady as I was, "and I didn't love him half as much as I love you."

And then his mouth was on mine again, and I held him to me, dizzy with... everything. Shock. Disbelief.

The deepest, most profound sense of relief I'd ever known.

I was breathless when I touched my forehead to his. "I love you, Cory. God, I... I have been in love with you for so long, I can't remember when I didn't."

"Me too," he whispered. "I don't know what it's like to not be in love with you."

My knees almost shook out from under me. "I'm so stupid."

"Yeah, well." He laughed. "So am I, apparently."

I managed a laugh, too, which felt damn good after the last however many hours.

"And for the record," he murmured, "everything you said about not being good enough for me?"

I drew back to meet his gaze. "Yeah?"

Cory ran his thumb along my bottom lip, and when he looked in my eyes, his were on fire. "You're out of your fucking mind."

The laugh that poured out of me felt amazing, but not nearly as amazing as Cory pulling me back in for another heart-stopping, all-consuming kiss.

Somehow it seemed apropos now that an angel and a demon had been involved in shoving our dumb asses together. We were both so damn oblivious, it really had taken some trickster magic and maybe some actual divine intervention to get us to see what was right in front of us.

And not a moment too soon, either.

He was breathing hard when he pulled back, and his eyes smoldered even hotter than before. "Any chance you want to pick up where we left off last night?"

Oh. Hell.

I licked my lips. Then I grinned.

And I was pretty sure he got the message.

CHAPTER 15

CORY

It was surreal to land in this bed with Matt again. Sinking onto the mattress with his amazing, naked body over mine was like coming home, like redemption, and like making love in a warzone—all at the same time. Last night hadn't even been that dramatic. There hadn't been a big battle or a screaming match. No one had said anything they couldn't take back. We'd both just made assumptions about each other, and when our emotions had slammed us both in the face, neither of us had known what to do, and we'd crashed and burned.

Now, after some of the longest hours I'd ever endured, we were back here. Matt was holding me like a life preserver, kissing me like he'd never tasted me before, and I was overcome with this profound feeling of being exactly where I needed to be. In his arms. In this bed. In this fledgling relationship that had been trying to get off the ground all this time.

Last night, I'd felt stupid for being that crushed after he'd—I thought—rejected me, but now I understood why it had been so hard to take. I'd had the briefest taste of being loved by Matt, and then I'd thought it had just been sex for him. Of course I'd been crushed.

And now...

God, it really had been love, and the taste I'd had last night was nothing compared to right now. Because right now, I knew. He'd said the words, and somehow I hadn't broken down crying, and I'd managed to say the same to him.

I loved him. He loved me.

This man who could've had anyone else he wanted... Who'd turned more heads than he'd realized at the club last night... Who should've had men knocking down his door for their shot with him...

He loved *me*.

Kissing and touching him now with our feelings out on the table was like nothing I'd ever experienced. It was fireworks, and it was the quiet calm of being home. Like this was the most spectacular moment of my life, but I was also settling into a place I belonged.

If I got through this without crying, it would be a genuine miracle.

And somehow, as I carded my fingers through Matt's hair and kissed him hungrily, I knew without a doubt that if I did break down, he'd just hold me and love me. He might even cry too.

We're here. We're home.

Matt broke the kiss and started down my neck, and I closed my eyes and tilted my head back. His lips lit up nerve endings like runway lights, and his soft, warm breath and rough chin on my skin had me gasping for air. How was it possible that all the fantasies I'd ever had about him were nowhere near as amazing as the real thing? That never happened.

Oh, but it was happening this time, and as Matt kissed his way down my neck and chest, I wasn't sure I could handle being this turned on. Only that I wanted to.

And then he was going down on me, licking and teasing me from base to head and back again, and I had to grab handfuls of sheets just to anchor myself in my bed.

"Holy fuck…" I stared down at him, trying not to come at the same time I tried to comprehend that *Matt Russo* was the one blowing me like there was nothing else in the world he wanted to do. He was definitely not one of those guys who sucked dick like it was a chore—he moaned around my cock, and every now and then he'd glance up and meet my eyes, arousal and hunger burning in his as he eagerly went to town on me.

"God, you're so good at that," I slurred. "Baby, your mouth…" I trailed off into a whimper, arching off the mattress as he fluttered his tongue over my balls. *"Fuuuck."* I wanted to return the favor. Switch, or sixty-nine—something. But he was just so damn good, I couldn't think enough to speak.

Finally, though, I found the breath and the brain cells to say, "My turn."

Matt gave my cock a slow lick, then met my gaze. "Yeah?"

"Uh-huh." I wiped a shaking hand over my face. "It'll… It'll give me a chance to calm down before I fuck you."

Interest sparked in his eyes, and he crawled up over me. "Maybe I want you to fuck me before you calm down."

I closed my fingers around his dick, reveling in the way he gasped and shuddered. "But I'll come too fast." I stroked him slowly. "And maybe I want you to be on the edge when I push into you."

Matt shivered, biting his lip. I didn't know how much of that was from what I was doing or what I'd said, but I liked it either way.

He rocked into my hand, groaning softly, then murmured, "Just fuck me. Or I'm... Jesus, if you go down on me, I'm going to come."

"Yeah?" I lifted my head and kissed him. "You make that sound like a bad thing."

"It's not." He chased my lips as I sank back to the pillow. "But I want to come with your dick in me."

It was my turn for a shiver. Holy fuck, his dirty mouth.

"You're not sore from last night?"

Matt shook his head, and an arrogant little grin came to life. "You didn't fuck me *that* hard."

I eyed him. "Is that a challenge?"

"Don't know. You up for it?"

"Get me a condom, and let's find out."

One more kiss, and he did exactly as he was told. I got up on my knees, and as I put on the condom, I nodded toward the pillow. "I want you on your back this time."

The heat in his eyes almost did me in. For the last few years, I'd wanted nothing more than to be the one turning him on, and now I was. Matt—my best friend, the man I'd secretly been in love with all this time—was gazing at me with hungry eyes, lying back on my bed with his legs spread wide for me, all but begging me to fuck him already.

Maybe one of these days, I'd tease him and make him *really* beg.

Not now, though. I needed him too much to play games.

So I didn't. I fingered him a little to make sure there was enough lube on both of us, and to make sure he was ready for me, and then I was doing exactly what I'd done in count-less fantasies—sliding my dick inside him while I watched his pleasure and need play out on his face. Oh, hell. Fantasies were nothing on the real thing. I'd imagined Matt turned on and pleading for my cock, but actually witnessing the speechless desperation, feeling his fingers digging into my thighs, hearing his whispered curses...

All I could think was that this moment was well worth all the time and frustration it had taken us to get here.

"You're so fucking gorgeous." The words tumbled out in a breathless rush. I had a split second to be irrationally sure he was going to laugh at me or roll his eyes, but the instant that lust-filled gaze met mine—nah, I wasn't worried. All this time, I'd wished he would look at me even once like I was someone who might pique his interest, and now he was staring up at me like he might eat me alive.

He swept his tongue across his lips and reached for me. "Come here."

I leaned down as best I could without folding him into a pretzel or pinching his balls between us. He pushed himself up on his elbow and met me halfway, curving a hand behind my neck as he kissed me in a way that said I did far, far more than pique his interest. No one had ever kissed me the way Matt did, and even now—tangled up and naked with him, balls-deep in him—I could still barely process that it was Matt kissing me and wanting me like this.

I was so caught up in the moment and his kiss, I almost forgot what else we were doing. My body remembered, though, and the need for friction had me rocking in and out of him. Not as hard as I'd planned or as he'd challenged, but pounding into him didn't feel right. Not this time. I just wanted to move in him. Move with him. *Feel* him.

He broke the kiss but kept a firm grip on my neck, and

his breath gusted across my lips as he said, "God, I love you."

A rush of emotion and elation almost knocked me off my stride, but I recovered quickly, and a second before I found his mouth again, I murmured, "I love you, too." I would never get tired of saying that. Or hearing him say it.

And it... didn't *hurt* to say it or think it anymore.

It shouldn't. Of course it shouldn't. But I'd been so frustrated and heartbroken for so long, just thinking it and wishing I could say it to him had hurt as if we were exes or something. As if every time the words ran through my mind, or even tumbled off my lips when I was alone, they cut a little deeper.

They didn't anymore. They were a salve now. A relief. Because I could finally say it to him, and he said it, too, and I *still* couldn't believe this was *real*.

If I thought too much about it, though, I'd wind up breaking down, and I didn't want to alarm Matt or ruin this moment.

Instead, I did the next best thing—gave him exactly what he wanted.

One deep thrust had him dropping back onto the bed with a startled "Oh, fuck," and I didn't give him a chance to recover before I did it again. Matt's eyes were wide, his lips apart, and he arched under me as I started railing him.

"You like that?" I asked.

The response was a choked whimper. He squirmed under me, rocking his hips to drive me one, and when he found his breath, he managed, "More. God, baby, *more.*"

His need was heady, his pleas absolutely music, and I fucked him for all I was worth. That chased away that certainty that my emotions were about to overwhelm me, and it also had us both groaning and cursing as my bed protested every hard, punishing thrust.

"Fuck, Cory..." He squeezed his eyes shut as he started pumping himself furiously. "Jesus Christ, that's so good."

"Yeah?" I bit my lip as I kept plowing into him. "Can you come like this?"

He moaned and arched. "I'm *gonna* come. God, keep... ungh, don't stop..."

As if he needed to tell me twice. I was too mesmerized to stop. By the physical sensation, but also the sheer rush of turning him into this. Watching him fall apart beneath me as I drove into him again and again and again. The flush of his skin. The muscles standing out on his arm and his abs. The way he tightened around me as we both sent him closer and closer to his orgasm.

Then his eyes flew open. He ground out a couple of curses, and then he let go of a cry that lit my senses on fire and nearly hauled me over the edge with him. His whole body quivered with the force of his climax, and cum dotted his abs as he mumbled absolute blissed out nonsense.

I rode him like a man possessed all the way through his orgasm, and it was that moment afterward—that sigh as he relaxed onto the bed, still trembling from his release—that made me let go. I forced myself in, shuddering hard, and I didn't even know what I was saying or if there were words at all as I came deep inside the man I loved.

With a ragged sigh, I slumped over him, shaking all over as I tried to hold myself up. Matt wrapped his arms around me and pulled me all the way down. He kissed my forehead, and then we were just still—panting, trembling, letting the ecstasy roll through us as the dust began to settle.

I was distantly aware that I'd been hurting earlier. That

I'd been sure Matt didn't want me for anything more than a roll in the hay.

In his arms now, as he stroked my hair and we caught our breath, I was as relieved as I was satisfied.

Matt didn't just want me physically. He loved me. He was holding me the way I'd always wished he could.

And everything was perfect.

CHAPTER 16

MATT

Magic was nothing unusual in my world. I spent more time around magic users than the average mortal, and I'd witnessed all kinds of things that most people never would. After fifteen years of representing sorcerers, fae, and the odd alchemist in the courtroom, it took a lot to shock or wow me.

And *nothing* had ever awed me more than this perfect, lazy moment in bed with Cory.

It was nothing short of a miracle that we were here. Him. Me. Naked. Satisfied. Completely in love. The man of my dreams who'd been right in front of me all this time in the form of the best friend I'd ever had.

Lying here with him, memorizing the shape of his body and the heat of his skin against mine as we shared languid kisses and blissed out looks, I was more content and awestruck than I'd ever been.

I'd done a lot of stupid shit in my life, but none of them would ever hold a candle to nearly losing him. Never making that mistake again, that was for sure.

I nuzzled his cheek and kissed him softly. "I love you."

His smile was everything. "I love you too." He ran his thumb along my lower lip. "I always have."

I was about to tell him I had too, but right then, a subtle zip of energy raised the hair on my neck. A flicker of movement from the corner of my eye turned my head, and somehow I wasn't surprised—and yet I was still startled—to see Andras and Raziel. Andras was sitting on the footboard. Raziel hovered beside him.

Disappointment tugged at me, and I held Cory closer, as if I was irrationally sure they'd come to tell me we couldn't be together. The fuck we couldn't. I'd walk around with those two on my shoulders till the end of time—professional and personal consequences be damned—if the alternative was letting go of Cory.

But the way Raziel smiled had me relaxing my grasp on my boyfriend.

"Well," he said. "I see our work here is done."

I snorted. "Uh-huh. He was right here this whole time, and you guys had me chasing every other man in the city."

"But you ended up here with him, didn't you?" Andras sounded impressively smug. "You think that was by accident?"

I stared at him, then exchanged puzzled glances with Cory.

Facing them again, Cory asked, "What are you talking about?"

Raziel's smugness matched Andras's now. "Matthew." He tsked and shook his head. "You really don't remember making this arrangement, do you?"

Some warmth rose in my face, though I wasn't sure why. "Um. I sort of do. Why?"

"You don't remember Bridget asking if there were any men in your life you could see yourself with?"

The warmth became an inferno. I could feel Cory's gaze on me, but I kept my own locked on Andras and Raziel.

"Is..." Cory whispered. "Is that how she knew I was your neighbor?"

And just like that, the memory snapped into place.

"There's one guy," I told her. *"A neighbor, actually. But we're just friends."*

"Oh?" She'd swirled her wineglass as she'd watched me intently. *"Tell me about him."*

I'd sighed, because there'd been nothing more frustrating than talking about my chronic solitude *and* my sweet, hot, gay neighbor. Drunk me had rambled on about him, too. *"You ever have one of those people you can go to about anything? Crisis? Breakup? Bored on a Saturday night? That's... I mean, I have no idea how he's still single. The guys he dates are just..."* I'd swung my glass around, nearly unloading its contents before taking a deep swallow. *"God, he deserves so much better than those asshats."*

"I'm sure he does," she'd said blandly. *"Maybe someone stable and smart?"*

"And just... not an asshole to him." I'd paused to roll a sip of Jack Daniels around in my mouth. *"He'll give the shirt off his back to anyone, and he'll bend over backwards to help anyone he cares about when they're in a crisis."* Sighing, I'd brought the glass up to my lips. *"Someone that good is way out of my league."*

In the present, I turned to Cory, meeting his confused expression. "I... told her I had this amazing neighbor who was sweet and gorgeous and way out of my league."

Cory's eyes widened. "What? Matt. I am so not out of—"

"You are," I whispered, smoothing his hair. "And I told her you'll help anyone you care about out of a crisis."

"So she *made* you a crisis," Raziel announced cheerfully. "And here you are!"

Cory chuckled. "That's her method, then? Send in her most incompetent pair to—"

"Incompetent?" Andras squeaked. "I *beg* your pardon?"

"I mean..." Cory shrugged. "*We* kinda did most of the work, didn't we?"

"Precisely." Raziel grinned. "And now look at you."

Cory and I exchanged puzzled looks.

Smugness radiated off Raziel as he said, "We're actually *very* good at what we do. And our assignment was to give him"—he nodded toward Cory—"a reason to shine as the man who knows you and loves you as well as he does."

My lips parted. When I turned to Cory, his jaw had gone slack. To the angel and demon, I said, "So this was— you guys were deliberately fucking up so he'd step in and get it right?"

They both looked exceptionally pleased with themselves as they nodded.

Cory laughed and leaned against me. "Man, I've heard of weaponized incompetence, but this..."

Rolling my eyes, I chuckled, wrapping an arm around him, and I kissed his temple. Yeah, it was devious as hell —*such* a shock with trickster magic involved—but I really couldn't complain about the results.

"We know what we're doing," Raziel insisted. "Just look at the two of you."

"Uh-huh," Cory said.

Raziel ruffled his wings and huffed, but then he said, "Well. We'll be off, then. Good luck, you two." I wondered if he noticed the startlingly fond way Andras looked at him right then, but before I could say anything, the demon just chuckled, shook his head, and looked away. And I thought *we* were idiots.

"Right," I said. "Uh, thanks for your help." Because hey, credit where it was due.

"You're most welcome," Raziel said.

Andras just gave a little grunt and an acknowledgment. As he pushed himself to his feet and flexed his wings, he said, "Bridget'll probably send you a survey about us and how we did." He flashed a shit-eating grin. "I trust you'll tell her the truth."

"Yeah, yeah." I laughed. "And then I probably get a coupon for ten percent off my next spell after completing the survey, right?" I rolled my eyes. "No, thanks."

He muttered something I didn't catch and snapped his wings. I chuckled. As relieved as I was that this spell was broken, I had to admit I'd miss some of their little idiosyncrasies. Life wasn't boring with them around, that was for sure.

The angel and demon exchanged glances and nods, probably readying themselves to depart. A glow started around them, similar to what I saw just before some of my fae clients vanished from my office.

"Oh, hey, Raziel?" I said. "One more thing."

They both turned. Raziel watched me curiously. Andras eyed me with a mix of annoyance and suspicion.

I grinned and gestured at Andras. "He's into you."

"What?" they both squawked. They turned to each other, shock registering across both their faces.

And in a blink of light, they were gone.

Cory laughed. "Did you just hook them up?"

I shrugged, pulling him closer to me. "Maybe? Or I just pissed off a demon. One of the two."

Curling his hand behind my neck, Cory murmured, "Hmm, I don't think you have to worry too much about that." He brushed his lips across mine. "And if he does show up with a vengeance, we can still order that electric flyswatter."

I laughed and buried my face against his shoulder. "Oh, God. I can just imagine presenting that to a judge." I kissed his collarbone. "Your Honor, my client didn't actually tase the demon. It was actually—"

Cory was shaking with laughter now, and I joined in. Holding him close, I let the humor wash over me along with the relief and the warmth of his body. Was I ever going to stop being stunned that we were here?

I hoped not.

I combed my fingers through his hair. "I can't believe it took me this long to figure out..." I shook my head as I trailed off.

Cory smiled, caressing my cheek. "To be fair, it took two to be this oblivious."

I snorted. "We're a great pair, aren't we?"

"Right?" He lifted his chin and dusted a soft kiss across my lips. "But we got here. That's all I care about."

Sobering, I nodded. "Me, too." It would probably take me a while to shake off the *oh shit* feeling, though. The realization of just how close I'd come to losing my chance with this man had left me jittery with adrenaline as if I'd narrowly avoided being hit by a speeding care. I didn't imagine I'd get over that any time soon.

And maybe I didn't want to. The lingering buzz of panic would make sure I never, ever took Cory for granted. I knew exactly how lucky I was to have him, and especially as long as my nerve endings still tingled with that hanging-by-my-fingernails fear, I wasn't going to forget it. That moment when he'd been so closed off, when he'd assumed I'd come for his trickster favor to get out from under my curse—no one had ever been further away from me.

Yet he'd still been willing to give me Galen's favor.

"You're incredible, you know that?" I whispered.

He peered curiously up at me. "Huh?"

"After last night, you were still going to give me that favor." I smoothed his hair as I swallowed hard. "Anyone else would've told me to pound sand."

Cory broke eye contact but didn't pull away from me. "It hurt. I'm not gonna lie."

Closing my eyes, I drew him in closer and kissed the top of his head. "I'm sorry."

"I know. And I understand now."

"But you were still going to let me use it."

This time, he did pull back, but only enough to look up at me. "You're still my friend."

"Even after—"

"Yes," he breathed. "I didn't just stop loving you because I thought you weren't into me."

"But you thought I used you."

He half-shrugged and didn't gainsay me. "Didn't mean I was going to turn my back on you."

I suspected he'd wanted to. The pain in his eyes when I'd come to his door—he'd probably wished he was the kind of person who could tell someone to get wrecked.

I was just incredibly fortunate he'd been willing to hear me out, and that I'd managed to soothe the hurt I'd caused him. All I had to do now was spend the rest of my life making up for it.

"I'm sorry," I said again. "I'm just glad you answered the door."

"Me too." He laughed halfheartedly. "I almost didn't.

But..." He sighed and met my gaze. "I don't know. Something told me I should."

"Good thing it did," I murmured, and claimed a kiss. There was nothing either of us could say that would soothe my conscience completely for hurting him like this, but the way he kissed me told me he really was moving forward. He was holding me tight, exploring my mouth in the most deliciously unhurried way, and like this, I could believe we were on solid ground.

How did I miss that you loved me?

Then again, he'd missed that I felt the same way, so maybe we really were oblivious idiots.

After a while, I broke the kiss and gazed into those beautiful eyes. "Okay. Question."

Cory lifted his chin. "Hmm?"

"How exactly did you wind up in possession of a favor from the Trickster King?"

He laughed, lighting up the whole damn world. "Oh. That. It's, um... The story isn't quite as exciting as you might think."

"Yeah?"

"Yeah. Basically, we were getting shit-faced with a couple of my clients, and—"

"Wait, wait, wait." I put up a hand. "Back up. How did you end up getting shit-faced with him? Because that's not exactly a minor thing, is it?"

"No. And that story isn't that impressive, either, honestly. He caught wind of me helping out several victims of a particular fae, and he was concerned about this being a trickster who'd gone rogue. Which... they had." Tsking, he rolled his eyes. "God, that was a shitshow. I mean, any other day, I'd have been like, 'whoa, wait, why the fuck is the Trickster King showing up in my office?' But that day, it was more like, 'Please tell me you're here to unfuck this mess.'"

"Which he was?"

Cory nodded. "That's a long, messy, and honestly boring story, because it was all red tape and bureaucracy and..." He waved his hand. Then he smirked. "Though, I'm pretty sure you get off on that kind of stuff?"

I rolled my eyes and elbowed him. "Shut up."

He snickered. "Okay. Anyway. So we finally got it all resolved and he got this trickster on a leash. Which—when the king shows up, most people fall into line, you know? So it was mostly a matter of fixing everything for my clients. Once that was done, we all ended up at a bar."

"I can buy that," I said. "I've gone out drinking with clients after a tough case." I paused. "Though I don't usually invite the judge along."

"Eh." Cory half-shrugged. "When the Trickster King says he's buying, and he promises *in writing* that there's no trickery and no strings attached? It'd be rude not to, you know?"

"Fair. So, you're all out drinking..." I raised my eyebrows.

"Right. And... I mean, we were all pretty lit. One of my clients could barely speak by this point, and I was slurring a little, but I could still speak coherently. So then the other client is all, 'Bet you can't say this when you're drunk.' And he has me read off some really complex city name in... I think it was Nepal? I don't remember."

I laughed. "And since you were all drunk, it escalated into trying to outdo each other?"

"More or less."

I could imagine that, especially since Cory was almost infuriatingly articulate when he was drunk. I'd forget how to pronounce my own single-syllable name, but he could sing karaoke drunk. Like, *hard* karaoke. Flawless-Gilbert-and-Sullivan-patter-song hard karaoke.

He shifted a little beside me, grinning. "So, the client was all flustered because I was making him look like an ass, and he looked up—you know that one village in Wales with the really long name?"

I grimaced. "God, I'd probably pull something trying to say that sober."

Cory chuckled. "Right, so he says he'll give me a hundred bucks if I can say it drunk. But then Galen, who is, like, fourteen sheets to the wind by this point, says that if I can do one more tequila shot and then pronounce it, he'll owe me a favor, to be cashed in at any time for anything."

I whistled. "Holy shit. And you must've nailed it, since you got the favor."

He beamed. "I've never been so happy to see a client so pissed off. Galen thought it was hilarious."

Shaking my head, I said, "So that's all it took? Saying that while you were hammered?"

"Hey, when the Trickster King gets drunk..." He offered up an innocent shrug.

I just laughed. "All right. So since you're sober, how do you say it?"

Cory grinned. "Llanfairpwllgwyngyllgogerychwyrn-drobwllllantysiliogogogoch."

I blinked. "Holy shit."

He looked about as smug as Raziel had. "What? You can't say it?"

"I... Christ, I couldn't even spell it."

Cory snorted. "Oh, don't ask me to spell it. But I can say it."

"So I gather. Llanfair..." I furrowed my brow, then shook myself. "Say it again? Slower?"

He grinned. Then, slower, he said, "Llanfairpwllgwyngyllgogerychwyrndrobwllllantysiliogogogoch."

I considered it, but just chuckled. "Okay, that's gonna be your party trick, not mine. Because... yeah, no."

No one in the world could be so simultaneously smug and endearing as Cory was in that moment, and I was pretty sure I fell for him all over again. As he slid closer to me, he said, "You don't have to say it. You just get to enjoy the benefits of me having such a limber tongue."

"Ooh, now you're speaking my language," I purred. "Does this mean you're good at tongue twisters, too?"

He laughed, and just before our lips met, he murmured, "Wouldn't you like to know?"

I would, yes. But it could wait.

Because right then, I was far more interested in his other oral talents.

He didn't seem to mind.

ACKNOWLEDGMENTS

Hat tip to Cynthia Diamond for letting me borrow Galen the Trickster King for a sort-of-cameo.

Visit Cynthia's website.

For more books by L.A. Witt, please visit

http://www.gallagherwitt.com

Romance * Suspense

Contemporary * Historical * Sports * Military

Titles Include

Rookie Mistake (written with Anna Zabo)

Scoreless Game (written with Anna Zabo)

The Hitman vs. Hitman Series (written with Cari Z)

The Bad Behavior Series (written with Cari Z)

The Gentlemen of the Emerald City Series

The Anchor Point Series

The Husband Gambit

Name From a Hat Trick

After December

Brick Walls

The Venetian and the Rum Runner

If The Seas Catch Fire

...and many, many more!

ABOUT THE AUTHOR

L.A. Witt is a romance and suspense author who has at last given up the exciting nomadic lifestyle of the military spouse (read: her husband finally retired). She now resides in Pittsburgh, where the potholes are determined to eat her car and her cats are endlessly taunted by a disrespectful squirrel named Moose. In her spare time, she can be found painting in her art room or destroying her voice at a Pittsburgh Penguins game.

Website: www.gallagherwitt.com
    Email: gallagherwitt@gmail.com
    Twitter: @GallagherWitt